NEVER

MIND

NIRVANA

NEVER

MIND

NIRVANA

A NOVEL

MARK

LINDQUIST

VILLARD ⚜ NEW YORK

Copyright © 2000 by Mark Lindquist

All rights reserved under International and Pan-American Copyright Conventions. Published in the United States by Villard Books, a division of Random House, Inc., New York, and simultaneously in Canada by Random House of Canada Limited, Toronto.

Villard Books and colophon are registered trademarks of Random House, Inc.

Library of Congress Cataloging-in-Publication Data

Lindquist, Mark
Never mind nirvana: a novel / Mark Lindquist.
p.   cm.
ISBN 0-679-46302-X (acid-free paper)
1. Young men—Washington (State)—Seattle—Fiction
2. Seattle (Wash.)—Fiction. I. Title.
PS3562.I51165 N48 2000   813'.54—dc21   99-088358

Villard Books website address: www.villard.com
Printed in the United States of America on acid-free paper
24689753
First Edition
Book Design by Jo Anne Metsch

For
Kerin Keller
Lisa Van Atta
Kim Warnick

ALL MY LIFE MY HEART HAS SOUGHT
SOMETHING I CANNOT NAME

—written on the men's room wall
of the Crocodile Cafe,
attributed to Chief Seattle,
probably incorrectly

NEVER

MIND

NIRVANA

Resurrection Jukebox

PETE TYLER is thirty-six years old. Or, as he has been saying since his birthday last week, *almost forty.*

He takes off his suit jacket and settles into the hammock with a copy of Richard Ford's *The Sportswriter,* a Vintage paperback he bought in his twenties because of the artwork—put him in mind of an album cover. Though he did not finish the book then, he thinks he will now. He is closer to the narrator's age. Concepts such as loss and regret have taken on meaning for him.

Tonight he plans to stay in and read for a change. He likes the idea of retiring into clean sheets by midnight, waking up without a hangover, knowing that the pubic hairs in the bed are his own.

However, after a few minutes Pete becomes restless. He wants to at least finish a chapter, but he thumbs forward and determines there are seventeen pages left, *too many.* He abandons Mr. Ford for the company of Johnnie Walker.

Glass in hand, he pulls up a stool in front of the stereo system stacked on milk crates, loads a six-disc cartridge into the CD player, cues up the Replacements' *Let It Be,* circa 1984. Friday night is traditionally Resurrection Jukebox night. Pete and many of his cohorts believe there is nothing more important or moving than a good rock-and-roll song, but fortunately this belief goes mostly unspoken.

His loft is eighteen hundred square feet of bouncy acoustics. The walls are whitewashed brick, floors are scuffed and scarred hardwood. Four twelve-by-five unwashed windows look out on Elliott Bay.

The simple bass riff of "I Will Dare" vibrates into Pete's chest and he lights an unfiltered Camel and nods along to Paul Westerberg, "*How young are you, how old am I, let's count the rings around my eyes . . .*"

Pete is vaguely aware that he is a little long in the tooth to be fixated on albums with song titles such as "Sixteen Blue," "Unsatisfied," and "Gary's Got a Boner," but he does not spend much time thinking about this. Pete prefers living to thinking. He has pressed on with this attitude despite mixed results.

Let It Be is followed by R.E.M., *Life's Rich Pageant,* circa 1986, with "These Days," "Fall On Me," and "Cuyahoga." Then he pulls out *Alice Cooper's Greatest Hits,* circa 1975, and listens to "I'm Eighteen," "No More Mr. Nice Guy," and the chestnut "Teenage Lament '74."

Next to Cooper is the Clash, *London Calling,* circa 1979, and after "Lost in the Supermarket," Pete clicks forward to "Train in Vain," the unlisted last track—"*you didn't stand by me . . .*"

By nine-thirty Pete is on his third glass of Johnnie and Pearl Jam's first album, circa 1991. During *Black* he starts to feel nostalgia and loneliness kicking in, just what he was trying to avoid.

He has Triscuits and salsa for dinner, replaces the suit pants with Levi's, loses the tie, slips on his old penny loafers. On the floor near his futon is a copy of *SPIN,* which he kicks under the *New York Times Book Review.* He hopes to make contact tonight with a girl who will be impressed by the latter, but knows he will more likely find someone familiar with the former.

Even more likely, he will be coming home alone, but who wants to plan for that?

Possibilities

PETE EXITS the building onto Western Avenue near the Harbor Steps. A light drizzle blows with the south wind and he faces away to light a Camel. He is trying to quit, but R.J. Reynolds is winning this battle.

Options for the night abound. To the south is Pioneer Square, several blocks of bars and clubs, known for a joint cover charge and a loudly social crowd. To the east are Gibson's and the Night Lite, alcoholic dives. To the north is the Belltown area, home to the Frontier Room, another alcoholic dive, Sit and Spin, a laundromat/bar/music venue, and also the Crocodile, where every decent Seattle band has played, as have many that are not.

Whichever route he chooses he knows he will carry with him the edgy suspicion he is missing something, that somewhere out there is the possibility he's been waiting all his life for and he is just not looking in the right place, *but one of these nights . . .*

The drizzle beads up on Pete's ragged blue blazer. He cups his cigarette, follows the street lamps north.

I Saw U

PETE MAKES his first stop at the Alibi Room, a well hidden bar in Post Alley just across from the Pike Place Cinema. He does not like the showy food, the screenplays on the shelves in lieu of books, or the frantic manager who scampers around in Nikes asking people to not use their cell phones. Pete comes here because of Carol.

"Hey," she says when he sidles up to the bar.

"Hey."

A Blur rip-off of a Pavement song plays on the house stereo as Carol shakes a martini. She wears hiphugger flares and a paint-spattered tank top that exposes the butterfly-and-roses tattoo on her chest. She's an artist.

Three months ago she invited him to a show at the Upchurch Gallery. Her paintings were black and abstract, indicative of a seriously disturbed personality. This intrigued Pete. He was unable to act on his interest, however, as she was busy pawing a boyfriend who resembled a young Elvis Costello. Pete could see they were in the initial infatuation stage.

"So what have you been up to?" Carol says as she brings him a shot of Johnnie Walker Black and a Pike Place Ale.

"Oh, just been worrying about the future."

She nods. "Did you hear about that poll where female White House staffers were asked if they would sleep with President Clinton? Ninety percent said 'Not again.' "

Pete smiles, nods. "Still seeing that guitarist?"

"When he's in town. He's touring now."

So he's probably picking up an STD as we speak.

"They're going through B.C.," she explains. "And then on to Toronto. They're very popular in Canada."

"When's he coming back?"

"Twenty-three days."

He cringes at the fact she's counting, downs the shot.

"He's been sending me these postcards and letters and cassette tapes," she continues, "and I'm making this collage for him and . . ."

Pete is willing to take on an incumbent if necessary, but he knows this can be expensive and time consuming, so he is waiting for an open seat.

On First Avenue he stops at Seattle's Best Coffee, which has replaced Fantasy Unlimited at the corner of Pike. Fantasy Unlimited sold dildos, cool postcards, and specialty clothing, including black leather bodysuits like the one worn by the Gimp in *Pulp Fiction.* Another local treasure lost to downtown development.

As he continues north, past the Champ Arcade—LIVE NUDE GIRLS!—he holds the double espresso with two hands and sips as he walks and the caffeine quickly kicks in with the alcohol and this low-grade speedball warms him.

The wind swirls into his face as he passes Market Place Tower. He considers a detour to the Pink Door in Post Alley, but decides he cannot deal with the color scheme, which is, unironically enough, primarily pink.

So he continues straight on and the Space Needle comes into view—the saucer-shaped restaurant on the top glowing blue and orange over the buildings ahead—and the sight gives him inexplicable comfort, his north star.

An unfamiliar bouncer guards the door of the Frontier Room and will not allow entry of the coffee cup. He also asks for I.D. Pete looks young for his age, but not that young. He sometimes worries that maybe he looks like some kind of law-enforcement agent.

Donna, the buff bartender, brings him a scotch before he asks. He tips her well.

"How come you haven't brought in any of those sweet young things lately?" she says.

"Because you'll steal them."

"A girl knows what a girl likes."

"I'm glad somebody does."

The obligatory banter accomplished, he sips the house scotch, which hits him like lighter fluid.

He makes a cursory scan for talent. Hardcore drinkers, once the exclusive occupants, have yielded the space to the music scene. Pete zeroes in on a striking waiflike girl, light skin, dark hair, nose stud. She is, however, already with a guy, and he looks vaguely like Chris Cornell from Soundgarden, but is actually Cornell's younger brother from Grace.

"Margaritas" by Love As Laughter plays on the jukebox. Though Pete appreciates the provincial emphasis on regional music of late, it reminds him that in the eighties you had to put a gun to the bartender's head if you wanted to hear a local band.

He shifts his reconnaissance into the pool-table room. Options appear limited, but he spots a possibility: pale Seattle skin with dark red lipstick, black bob, glasses. Five people sit at her table, two other women, two guys, not coupled up. Next to her beer is an empty shot glass, and she is draining a pint of what appears to be Heffeweizen in long gulps. Two good signs. He sets up a stakeout.

Picking up a copy of *The Stranger*—"Free Every Thursday!"—from a table in the hallway within eyesight of his target, he opens to the "I Saw U" section.

EROTIC DAY GIRL @ CHA CHA 3/10

U: "Have an Erotic Day" T-shirt. Me: blond hair, blackly clothed. Eyes kept meeting. But you left with poser. Single? Coffee? Heroin?

HARVEY DANGER @ SIT AND SPIN

Valentine's Day. U: green/pink/black hair. I said, "Nice hair." Trying to flirt. Failed. Let me try again? "I'm not sick but I'm not well."

He skims ads with headlines such as ART GIRL, MINNIES ON DENNY, BILL'S ON BROADWAY, and KISS ME ON THE BUS. He religiously reads this section of *The Stranger*. He is moved by these screams into the void.

Meanwhile, Drinking Girl With Glasses finishes her beer. As she glances around for a waitress, she sees him looking her way. Eyes meet. Hers dart away. He looks back down at the paper.

She stands. He keeps his nose in *The Stranger* until he senses her approaching. He looks up, feigns surprise at the sight of her, smiles.

She returns the smile, and walks on by.

He waits a couple beats, then follows her to the bar. She is wearing a black skirt and her legs are bare, a bold choice for the schizophrenic season between winter and spring. He cuts around her, catches Donna's eye.

Donna responds with a quick scotch on the rocks.

"What are you drinking?" he asks Drinking Girl as he pulls out his wallet.

She hesitates, then says, "Heffeweizen."

"And a Heffeweizen," he repeats to Donna as he pays.

"Thanks," Drinking Girl says.

"You're welcome."

"So," she says, "are you from around here?"

"Born and raised."

"I just moved here. Got a job at Amazon.com. Figured it was time to get a real job since it's the last year of the millennium and all."

"Actually next year is the last year of the millennium."

"Huh?"

"Two thousand is the last year of the millennium."

Blank stare in response.

"Because the first year of the millennium was 1901," he explains. "So 2000 is the last year. Two thousand and one is the first year of the next millennium. That's why Kubrick called his movie *2001*, instead of *2000*."

She still stares blankly at him and he realizes he is totally losing her.

"Where are you from?" he tries.

"Vancouver."

"B.C.?"

"Washington."

"Well, welcome to Seattle."

The beer arrives and they touch glasses in a toast.

"My friends and I are thinking of going to the Crocodile," she says. "You know that place?"

He nods, decides not to mention that he has spent approximately forty-two percent of his adult life there.

"Maybe I'll see you later then?"

He smiles, nods.

Outside, the drizzling rain has let up and a nearly full moon is rising between light cirrus clouds over the Bank of America Building. The sidewalks are filling with nightlife. Pete notices every couple, wonders what the guy has done to get the girl.

He passes the Bethel Church on Lenora and Second. The ever-changing marquee reads: LET JESUS BE YOUR RHYTHM SECTION. Further evidence in Pete's mind that too many musicians are still moving here.

Outside the Crocodile Cafe, Pete steps in line behind two guys, one in a suit and the other in a leather jacket. A scan of the flyers on the glass door indicates that the Murder City Devils and Tight Bros From Way Back When play tonight, good news. Kevin, the doorman, spots Pete and waves him past, a small courtesy Pete appreciates.

He strolls through the dining area and doesn't see anyone he knows, so he follows a guy with a black and green Crocodile BE-HAVIOR MONITOR T-shirt who clears a trail down the hallway.

In the back bar the haphazardly arranged tables and booths are full. Among the junk that passes for decor are chandeliers, neon bars, papier-mâché crocodiles, and sheep with wings hanging from the ceiling. Pete is, as always, disturbed by the winged sheep. If they were pigs, he would understand.

He locates an empty bar stool and thereby avoids the drink line. Jennifer, the bartender, brings him a Johnnie Walker Black. She is cool and pretty and too many people hit on her so Pete does not.

"Did you hear Beth's back in town?" Jennifer says.

"What?"

"Beth Keller. She's apparently back in town."

Pete spent three months living with Beth in a motel thirteen years ago and has not seen her since. He calls those the best weeks of his life, at least when he is drunk.

Stephanie, the owner, steps out from the EMPLOYEES ONLY passage and gives Pete a quick wave. She is tall and stunning and wearing red lipstick, but unavailable, married to a rock star from Georgia who recently moved to Seattle. They have children, which impresses Pete.

"Jennifer," he calls out as she pours a draft for another customer.

"Yeah?"

"Did you see her?"

"Who?"

"Beth."

"No, I just heard she was around."

Pete lights a Camel, drinks his scotch. Estimated bloodalcohol: .05 and rising fast. A guy pulls up next to him wearing a SEATTLE THINKS THE REAL WORLD SUCKS T-shirt. Pete thinks this ought to go without saying.

Recognizing the noise of a band taking the stage, Pete dismounts from his stool. He enters the employees' GO door, passes through a narrow room that always puts him in mind of Bobby Kennedy's assassination, and emerges in the live music area. He finds space by the sound booth and leans back against the wall.

The sound mix is muddy—the air is moist with breath and sweat and smoke and so the high ends are muted. The sound tech has not compensated for this. He is probably on drugs, and not the right ones.

The crowd, however, does not mind. Spencer steps up to the

edge of the stage and grabs the mike stand—"*I never want you to be a sailor's girl*"—and he leans over the gals in front and their hands flail up at him and his sweat and spit shine in the white spotlight.

Though Pete cannot understand half of the lyrics, Spencer acts like he means it, and the band looks like they're enjoying it, and this taps into a mix of emotions for Pete—he misses the stage, misses those moments, but would rather not, does not, will not, think about this.

He spots a possibility leaning against a wall: tall, hyperthin, no makeup. Most of the young crowd has pushed up front toward the mosh pit and so it is not too jammed in the back near the bar. Pete edges in her direction, acting as if he is trying to find a good sight line to the stage.

When the Devils take a tuning break, Pete decides to make a move. He is not quite drunk enough to say "Come home with me and the material world will melt and it won't matter if God is dead," so he just says, "Hi."

"Hi."

"What do you think?"

"I've seen them when they were too fucked up to stand, so I'd say they're doing great tonight."

Pete takes this abundance of information as meaning she is amenable to conversation. He glances at the half-empty glass in his hand. "Want to go get a drink?" he asks.

"Thanks. But I'm waiting to hear this new song Derek said they would play for me."

Derek would be Derek Fudesco, the bass guitarist.

Back in the dining area, Pete spots a girl eating a veggie Reuben sandwich by herself, reading *The Stranger*. She wears an abundance of rings, but nothing matrimonial.

Pete boozily stares. Girl With Rings remains oblivious. He sips at his beer without taking his eyes off her. Eventually she senses something, looks over, gives him absolutely nothing, returns to *The Stranger*. He looks away, then checks back to see if she does a double take.

Nope.

Pete generally looks for some sign of encouragement, as this, he believes, is among the subtle qualities that distinguish him from a stalker. Seeing none, he moves on.

At the bar he orders another scotch from Jennifer. Kurt Cobain, wearing rose-colored glasses, stares at Pete from a framed photograph above the cash register.

"Who told you Beth was in town?" Pete asks when his drink arrives.

"Hadley, I think. I'm not sure."

He feels the doom of two A.M. upon him and knows all the misery flesh is heir to awaits him at home.

Lying in bed alone and thinking of Beth and all the accompanying regret is one of the worst ends to a night he can imagine, but he knows a lost cause when he is one.

As he's about to step out the south side exit, he spots Drinking Girl—she's weaving down the narrow hall that separates the bar from the dining area and she smiles and waves at him like he's a long-lost friend.

"Are you leaving?" she asks.

"Well . . ."

"Let's have a drink." She tugs him away from the door.

At the bar he turns to her, "Heffeweizen?"

"Guinness."

"Weren't you drinking Heffeweizen earlier?"

"Oh," she says, "and a shot of Jägermeister."

They sit at bar stools and form an alcohol-soaked bond discussing movies and music and the too many people moving to Seattle. In the course of this he learns her name is Rose, born in Renton, biological father left when she was twelve, hates her stepfather—hints of domestic violence—she went to public schools, dropped out of the University of Washington, tried heroin, liked it so tried to avoid it, has stock options at Amazon.com.

Rose does not seem to be conscious of how high her black skirt rides up her thighs. She does seem to be conscious of how she flicks her tongue stud on her teeth, which, Pete notes, are good. She actually looks better than Pete remembers from the Frontier Room and he does not attribute this to alcohol.

"Last call," Jennifer announces.

Time just keeps ticking away.

Rose turns to Pete, "Last call? *Already?*" She sounds heartbroken.

"There's plenty more booze at my place," Pete says. "And some good CDs." He tries not to sound like she is his last likely hope of getting laid tonight. "Just a few blocks from here. Bar never closes."

She appears to be considering, just needs a push.

"The Oceanic Building," he adds, as though this might make a difference.

"I should probably check with my friends."

"Where are they?"

"I don't know." She laughs.

"I have Jägermeister in the freezer."

They walk south on Second Avenue, slurring their feet, hips bumping into each other. Pete hails a Yellow Cab at Pine as rain starts falling.

"You're not an ax-murderer or anything," Rose says as the taxi pulls over, "are you?"

"Not as far as you know."

Courtney Love Must Die

"COOL," ROSE says when they enter Pete's loft.

Pete suspects that part of what women are weighing when deciding whether to sleep with a guy is the feel of the total experience. Men will have sex in an outhouse. Women, however, tend to be more sensitive to their surroundings. Pete's ascetic loft space has a good feel and, additionally, it's an advertisement for untapped potential.

Rose steps to the west windows, almost tripping on one of the uneven floor planks. The moon shines through broken clouds over Alki Beach as the last ferry run of the night crosses Elliott Bay toward Bainbridge Island with the porthole lights of the white and green double-ended ship reflecting off the dark water.

"What a view," she says. "I could spend hours just staring. Smoking a joint and just staring."

He checks out her legs and ass, thinks well of both.

She turns to him. "Hey, do you have any pot?"

"No, sorry."

She looks around the space, takes in the rolling racks of white shirts and dark suits, the hundreds of CDs and books stacked on the floor, the futon, the hammock, and not much else.

"Did you just get divorced or something?" she asks.

"Never been married."

"How long have you lived here?"

"About seven years."

"Are you an artist? What do you do?"

Pete pauses to light a Camel. This should not be a perplexing question, but Pete always wrestles with the issue of how much information he must reveal.

"I used to be in a band," he says, "but now I'm a lawyer."

"What band?"

"Morph."

" 'Quaalude Fellatio'?"

"Yep."

She stares at him. "You were the singer, played bass?"

"The one without any musical talent."

"Oh, yeah. *Wow*. I remember you guys. You and Todd and what's-his-name. Didn't somebody die?"

"Bob."

"Overdose?"

"Yeah."

"Do you think you might get back together?"

"Bob is dead," he reminds her.

"You can always replace a drummer."

Pete has made this same unfortunate comment to Todd, and he suddenly realizes how it must have sounded. He opens a window a crack, flicks his cigarette into the empty street where it explodes into orange embers before fizzling out in the wetness.

"And now you're a *lawyer*?"

He nods. "I'll put on some music."

"Where's your bathroom?"

He points her in the general direction, then crosses to the stereo. He weighs Hole's *Celebrity Skin* against a Mother Love Bone compilation with "Chloe Dancer/Crown of Thorns." Pearl Jam is another possibility, as Eddie Vedder often puts Seattle girls in the mood. Pete decides on Hole, reasoning that it is most conducive to the reckless atmosphere necessary for sex with a near stranger.

Courtney's hollering drowns out the traffic noise from the Alaskan Way Viaduct. "*Oh, make me over . . .*"

Pete pulls ice and Jägermeister out of the freezer, which is not self-defrosting and therefore looks like an arctic winter inside. He pours a Johnnie Walker Black on ice and a shot of Jäger.

Rose returns from the bathroom, no longer wearing her glasses. She stops in the middle of the room and stares at his KEF speakers. "Courtney Love must die," she announces, then climbs into the hammock. Suddenly she reaches her arms to the sides, presumably to stop the swinging. She is not well schooled in physics.

Pete steps over and stops the hammock, then offers her the shot.

Rose sits up, looks at him, vomits.

The spray, which Pete watches in what seems like slow motion, cascades across his left leg on its way toward an unpleasant splash on the floor.

She then tries to climb out of the hammock. He fears she is going to fall, so he grabs her to help, spilling the Jägermeister in the process. Her second retching goes mostly over his shoulder, but the follow-up spit dribbles down his back.

"Are you okay?" he says, senselessly.

"I'm okay," she says, just as senselessly.

He gently holds her up on her feet. Suddenly she is dead weight.

"Throw up some more," she says.

"Not yet," he suggests.

He helps her to the bathroom, where she lies down and curls around the toilet. Pete notices the red panties as her skirt hikes up and he looks longer than he should, given the circumstances.

"You want some water?"

She shakes her head, groans, then stretches out flat on her back, eyes closed.

"Rose?"

No answer.

"Rose," he repeats.

She says nothing, but it is evident from the movement of the puke bubbles on her lips that she is still breathing. Pete picks her up by putting his arms under her shoulders. Walking backwards, he carries her toward the kitchen, her feet leaving trails on the dusty floor. Rose makes some noises that suggest she does not want to be moved, but she is not in a strong position to protest.

Suddenly the phone rings. His answering machine picks up and he can hear a voice competing with Courtney. "Hi, it's me. Just got off work. Are you there?"

Me is Winter, so named by her hippie parents, and *work* is the Lusty, a peep show just across Post Alley from the Oceanic Building.

"Who's that?" Rose perks up.

Pete desperately wants to speak with Winter at this moment, but does not want to literally drop Rose.

"Okay," Winter says, "guess you're not picking up. You probably have some slut over there. Call me later."

"Why does she say she's not selling sheep?" Rose asks. "I don't get it. Why would she be selling sheep?"

After a beat Pete realizes Rose is referring to the song lyrics. "*Cheap,*" he explains. "The line is 'I'm not selling *cheap.*' "

"Oh."

Pete slowly props Rose up so she can stand on her own. He puts his arm around her waist and walks her over to the kitchen counter island, which she leans shakily against.

He pours a glass of water from the tap and holds it out. Rose takes it with both hands and drinks. When she finishes, he takes the glass back before she can drop it.

"Sorry," Rose slurs as she wipes her nose. "I probably didn't need the heroin."

Snorting up in the bathroom, great. "*I have no idea where she got the heroin, Officer.*"

"How much did you do?"

"Not much. There was just a teeny bit left."

"Are you going to throw up again?"

"No. I don't think so."

He flashes on the image of her exposed flesh and panties in the bathroom, wonders if the night can be salvaged.

She turns her head toward him, seems to slowly focus. "I should get home. Could you drive me?"

"I probably shouldn't drive right now."

"Why not?"

"Well, I think I've been drinking too much."

"I don't mind."

Pause.

"I'll call a taxi," he says.

In the freight elevator she collapses to the floor. He lets her lie there until he stops the elevator and opens the vertically sliding doors. Then he picks her up and walks her out to Western and University, where, he vaguely remembers, this travesty of an evening started with the usual unjustified bright expectations.

Just lost another night you'll never get back.

The moon has slipped into the western horizon, just over the snow-peaked Olympic Mountains. A ferry sits quiet at the dock, still lit up. Traffic on the usually busy Alaskan Way Viaduct is sporadic.

He helps her sit on the curb. He lights a cigarette and the wafting tobacco smoke partially overcomes the stench of vomit.

When the Pioneer taxi arrives, Pete gives the cabbie the address on Rose's driver's license and a twenty. He then loads her into the backseat like a sack of Idaho potatoes.

"You'll forget about all of this tomorrow," he says, wishing he could say the same for himself.

Future Tense

"MOTHER, I'M almost forty."

"You're thirty-six, Peter."

"Almost forty. Time's been speeding up since I quit doing drugs."

"That's just because you're getting older. Don't make it sound like you were an addict."

Pete did enough drugs in his twenties to make Marilyn Manson blush. Still, his mother refuses to acknowledge his youthful preference for the depraved. The years he spent in the band go mostly undiscussed.

On his knees, with a ruler and pencil, Pete sketches a twelve-by-eight-inch outline on a side door of the house. His mother stands over him with a glass of wine.

"So, if you're thirty-six," his mother says, "Sandy must be thirteen."

Sandy is his parents' third dog. The first two, Missy and then Sid, were golden retrievers. Sid died after Pete and his sister left home. Their father declined to buy another. Mother, however, took a liking to an abandoned pup at a QFC grocery store on Sand Point Way. This happened just before Pete moved back in with his parents to rest after a tour, the tour he met Beth Keller on. Sandy always reminds Pete of that time and he cannot think of that time without thinking of Beth.

Pete puts down the pencil and ruler and picks up an electric circular saw.

"You sure she'll fit through there?"

"It's a medium," he says.

"Perhaps you should have bought a large."

"Those are for Saint Bernards."

"As Sandy's been getting older she's been getting a little, well, *rounder*." His mother looks at Sandy with an apologetic expression.

Pete starts the saw. "Hold her back, please."

"It looks small," she says, taking Sandy's collar.

Pete presses the blade to the pencil outline and sawdust flies.

"Watch your fingers," his mother says over the noise.

He cuts four straight lines and as he completes the last one a rectangle falls out.

"Looks small," his mother repeats.

He unplugs the saw, sets it down. Sandy approaches to sniff the handiwork.

Pete opens the door, steps inside, closes the door.

"Sandy," he calls.

She pokes her head through the hole.

"Come here." He pats his thigh.

Sandy shimmies through, smiles at Pete, and then turns and shimmies back out, apparently grasping the concept.

"It's a little *snug*," his mother says from the other side. "But it looks like it will do, thank you."

Pete walks into the kitchen. The low afternoon sun shines through the picture window, warms the room. He pulls a Rainier out of the refrigerator and sits at a bar stool and looks out at the beer's namesake mountain dominating the southeastern horizon. The back lawn slopes down to Lake Washington and the afternoon breeze carries traffic noise from the I-520 floating bridge, which his mother calls "the new bridge," though it was completed in 1963.

She enters and pours herself another glass of Ste. Michelle

Chardonnay. Sandy comes in behind her and licks at something on the pinewood floor.

"Do you remember Beth?" Pete asks.

"Beth? Was she the Canadian?"

"No. That was Jayne. Right time period, though."

"Beth was the tall girl with dark hair?"

"No, that was Sarah. Beth was the one who moved to L.A. She called here a few times?"

"Oh, yes. Right." She sits next to him. "I never met her, but I remember you talking about her."

"I hear she's in town."

"You've stayed in touch?"

"No."

"Oh."

"Do you think I should try to contact her?"

"Well, that might be nice."

"You don't think it might seem weird?"

"Why should it be weird?"

"I don't know," he says. "It's been more than ten years."

"What does she do now?"

Depends who you believe. "I'm not sure."

"Is she married?"

"I doubt it."

"She'll probably be happy to hear from you."

"Maybe." His stomach reacts to this conversation and he takes a long drink of the beer. He is craving a cigarette, but does not smoke in front of his mother. Long ago he told her he quit.

"Are you still dating that young woman?"

"Which one?"

"The one with the peculiar name."

"Winter?"

"Right."

"Yes. Yes, I am."

"Are you bringing her to Katie's party?"

Pete shakes his head.

"I'd like to meet her."

"I don't want to bring her to a birthday party for my sister's four-year-old."

His mother nods. "Okay. We could have a barbecue here. Or go out for dinner?"

"What?"

Pete's hearing is permanently damaged from the Bad Old Days. Still, sometimes he says "what" just to avoid answering questions. His mother is familiar with this transparent routine and waits for an answer.

"I'll talk to her about it."

"I think it's a little funny that you've been seeing her for a few months and neither Katie nor I have met her."

"She has an unorthodox schedule."

"What does she do?"

"She's kind of in the arts."

"Are you serious about her?"

"Serious? I don't know."

"You don't know?"

"No."

Pause.

"Do you think you might settle down at some point, Peter?"

Pete shrugs. His mother has been uncharacteristically philosophic of late. They never used to talk about personal matters but lately they have been, and this is not Pete's strong suit.

"Don't you ever worry about the future?" she asks.

He nods. "I do."

"Well, do you want to be single your whole life?"

"I don't think so."

"Do you think there's possibly a *reason* why you're still single?"

"Probably."

"Do you know what it is?"

"Luck?"

"Maybe you want too much."

"Maybe."

"If you want too much," his mother says, "you can end up with nothing."

Pete nods. He bends down and scratches Sandy's neck. "I should finish the dog door and clean up," he says. "Then I have to go."

He does not want to be here for the sunset. Sunsets of late have been as disturbing for him as a falling guillotine.

"I suppose it's fun to be single when you're young," his mother says. "Sometimes I wonder what that would have been like." She takes a drink. "But I'll tell you one thing for sure: you don't want to grow old alone."

In this, too, he suspects his mother is right.

Welcome to the Working Week

PETE BRIEFLY flashes his badge and I.D. card as he cuts around the line for the metal detector at the downtown courthouse entrance. Nobody even glances at his I.D. They apparently do not realize he does not really belong.

He is not paying attention to the usual crowd of lawyers, defendants, and civilians when he steps to the back of the elevator. On the second floor, however, Pete catches the smell of Chanel perfume and looks up to see a beautiful fair-skinned Scandinavian woman enter.

She is blond with green eyes and is holding a double Starbucks in the classic Seattle two-hand coffee-sipper's grip. Wearing Levi's and a Shetland sweater, she is not a lawyer, probably not a defendant.

As the door closes she steps against the east wall, displaying a fine profile. She senses him staring at her and turns.

Pete smiles. She smiles back, neutrally.

He could try the old "Looking for the infraction windows?" line. Though last time he used this line the woman said, "No, I'm just here for my boyfriend's arraignment."

On the sixth floor she steps out. Pete watches her walk away, hoping for an over-the-shoulder glance. The doors close. Still, his spirits lift because the sight of an attractive woman always reminds him: *possibilities*.

He exits on the ninth floor, punches the code on the office security door, and walks down the hallway of the Sexual Assault Unit, which is lined with Disney cartoon posters for the benefit of child victims. The caricatures strike Pete as surreal and sometimes creepy.

His office door is papered with pages of police reports, particularly entertaining passages highlighted with yellow accent markers. Pete's current favorite is a quote from a trailer-park rapist who preferred underage girls, especially cousins:

> *I placed the defendant under arrest and read him his rights. When I asked him if he understood, he said, "What does a girl in Eatonville say when she loses her virginity?" I asked him again if he understood and he replied, "She says GET OFF ME, DAD, YOU'RE CRUSHING MY SMOKES!"*

There are no diplomas on the wall, no certifications, no proof of his acceptance into the Washington State Bar Association. Pete figures this is not necessary as he could not be a deputy prosecutor without the requisite degrees and acceptance into the bar, so why does he need proof?

The only things in frames are the two office awards he won early in his career for "Trial Attorney of the Year," which sit on a bookshelf. He keeps these because he is proud of them and because he needs to glance at them occasionally to assure himself he did not make a bizarre mistake by becoming a prosecutor.

Trial work came easily to Pete. Still, he has doubts. He was twenty-seven years old, *almost thirty,* when he took stock of his situation and decided he did not want to be in his thirties or, worse, his forties, and struggling along with an overgrown grunge band. In the rare moments he tried to picture his future he saw images of himself old and alone and broke and addicted, and it chilled him with absolute fear. Also, Mick Jagger made him want to puke.

On the other hand, he was not in a rush to grow up. When in doubt, he figured, stall.

So he went to law school. Jesus wept.

Seven years later and Pete still has not made a full commitment to the transition from his extended adolescence. He has not adjusted to the fact that he has an office. He even tries not to think of it as an office, but just as a backstage area for hanging out.

Consistent with this harebrained fiction, he spends a lot of time in his old leather chair listening to Andy Savage and Steve the Producer on 107.7 and drinking coffee and staring out the window at the Safeco Field construction. This is what he is doing when Detective Bradley Tuiaia enters and drops a thick police report on the desk.

"Norm and Satterblack are both completely senile," Tuiaia says, "so I talked to John about this case and we agree—it's got your name on it." The thirty-year-old detective is a former UW linebacker, a stocky half-Samoan known for his aggressive streak. He and Pete have worked well together on past cases. "Take a look," he says, gesturing to the report.

"I don't like reading this early in the A.M."

"I'll give you a synopsis."

"Is it a kid case?"

Tuiaia shakes his head. "Adult rape."

"Okay."

The detective starts talking with Soundgarden's "Burden in Hand" playing. "Victim's eighteen, defendant's thirty-five. They meet at a bar, the Breakroom on Capitol Hill. They know each other, have a few common friends, but no sexual history together. Last call comes and he invites her back to his place, where they can keep drinking. Once again, our state's two A.M. cutoff for alcohol factors into a date rape."

"She's eighteen and they met at a bar?"

"Fake I.D."

"Beautiful."

"They keep drinking at his place, then decide to watch a video. The TV is in the bedroom, so they lie down on the bed to watch. He takes off his clothes, down to his skivvies, and climbs under the covers. She asks to borrow a T-shirt and gets in bed with that and her panties still on. He loses interest in the movie about this time, starts groping her. She says she kisses him back at first, but then his hands go straight to her crotch and she pulls his hands away. Things start to escalate here. He tries to pull her panties down with one hand, but she pulls them back up, and then he uses both hands and pulls them down. She's fighting, kicking her legs, trying to pull them back up, but he gets them off. He's about six foot, maybe one-seventy. She's fairly tall for a girl, but really skinny. Once he's got her panties off he pulls down his skivvies and climbs on top of her. He tries to penetrate her at this point. She's screaming by now. At first he's got her hands pinned above her head, using both his hands, one hand on each of her wrists, but she's kicking her legs and wiggling her hips. So he lets go of her wrists and grabs her legs, wrestles them apart. Her hands are free now and she punches and slaps him in the head and face area, but he just ducks and takes the blows. With his hands holding her legs he finally penetrates her and starts going at it. Once he's inside her, she digs her nails into his shoulders, hard as she can, but he keeps going, and she just kind of gives up. But then she realizes something and says to him, 'You're not even wearing a condom.'

"And he actually stops. He gets off her and reaches over to his nightstand, apparently to get a condom. Once he's off, though, she runs into the bathroom, locks the door behind her. She's panicked. She sits on the floor, back to the door, her legs up against the toilet for leverage if he tries to break in the door. But nothing happens for a couple minutes.

"Then, after a while, he knocks. And suddenly he's all apologetic, first thing he says is, 'Hey, that wasn't very cool of me.' He blames it on the booze, downplays it. He asks her to unlock the door. At first she doesn't. But he keeps apologizing, finally talks her into opening the door."

Tuiaia takes a seat. "And here's the problem."

Pete waits. "Burden in Hand" segues into Matchbox 20's "Push," two good songs with semi–domestic-violence themes, and Pete resists commenting on this.

"He somehow talks her into coming back to bed. She said she didn't know what else to do. Anyway, they both go to sleep, or pass out. She wakes up early, while it's still dark out, and manages to leave without waking him. Her roommate is home by the time she gets back to her apartment and she tells her what happened. The roommate tells her to report it immediately. But she doesn't. She takes a shower and climbs into bed and falls asleep. She doesn't get up until about noon. And she still doesn't call the police. But she calls a rape hotline. And the rape counselor talks her into reporting this. Enter yours truly. I go over to her place and she tells me what I told you. I asked her for her underwear. They were ripped and stretched. I told her to go to the hospital for a rape exam, though it was probably too late to be of much use."

"What kind of witness will she make?"

"She's kind of shy, young, good looking in that Capitol Hill punk way. She'll clean up well."

"What's the guy have to say?"

"First I talked to some people who were at the Breakroom that night, including this somewhat respectable guy named Chad who's the booking agent, and he confirmed that the victim and the defendant left together. So I went to his apartment. About ten o'clock Sunday morning. Woke him up. I asked him if he knew what I was doing there. He said he had no idea. I asked him if he was with Amber Nickerson on Friday night. He said, 'Who?' I repeated her name. He said, 'Maybe.' I just stared at him. Then he said, 'Okay, yeah.' I asked him if they left the Breakroom together. He paused, then said, 'Yeah.' I asked him if she came home with him. He paused again, this time for about ten seconds, then said, 'Do I need to talk to a lawyer?' "

Pete groans.

"I gave the standard, 'It's up to you, I can't give you legal advice.' " Tuiaia smiles for the first time. "I may have added something about how I was just there to get his side of the story, but, *hey if you don't want to tell me your side of the story . . .*' And he decided to talk.

"He told me essentially the same things she did, except he said that she was into him, but they didn't have intercourse because she wanted him to wear a condom and he couldn't find one. I asked him about the bruising that was starting near his eye. He didn't know where that was from. He volunteered that he often wakes up with bruises after drinking.

"Anyway, he agreed to come down to the station for a taped statement. And get this: in the taped statement, he said something new—said that they actually *did* have intercourse, and it's *possible* it wasn't consensual—"

"Possible?"

"That's as far as he would admit. He kept falling back on how drunk he was. He said it was possible that it wasn't consensual, but he was really drunk, and his memory is vague. But he's sure he stopped when she asked him to wear a condom and he couldn't find one. Sounded like he was worried we might be able to prove they had intercourse, so he decided to admit it. After we finished the statement, I thanked him, then arrested him."

"There's something you're not telling me here."

"No, that pretty much sums it up."

"Then why do you want me to handle this case?"

"You're the best at selling whacked victims to juries. I've heard you explain things like delays in reporting, continued contact, all the textbook reactions. You understand the psychology of this stuff." The detective grins.

"Don't bullshit me. Scott or anyone else in the unit could handle this like a cakewalk."

Tuiaia points to the police report. Pete picks it up and reads the defendant's name: JOHNSON, KEITH E.

Oh, shit.

"It's your old world, Pete."

Scott Foss

PETE STEPS over several books and notebooks on the floor as he enters Scott Foss's office. Scott slowly turns his head away from the computer screen, squints.

"Good morning," Pete says.

"What's up?"

"You sick?"

"Hungover. Think I'd blow about a .07 on a PBT. Had a date with some new last night." Scott uses *new* as a noun.

He is several years younger than Pete, deceptively clean-cut, good in trial, and was twice voted Most Likely to Lose His Job Because of Criminal Charges at the annual holiday party.

Pete sets the Keith Johnson file on the desk among several other files scattered in no discernible order.

"Do I need to look at that?" Scott asks.

"You're handling the arraignment this afternoon. It's a Rape 2. Date rape without the date."

"Am I second-chairing this?"

"Yeah, but don't say anything to the press yet."

"The press?" Scott starts to wake up. He pours himself a cup from an old Mr. Coffee.

"Defendant is Keith Johnson. A.k.a. Keith Junior."

"The guitarist?"

"Yeah."

"You know him?"

"Only vaguely," Pete says. "Our bands overlapped in the late eighties, but mine went to L.A., his stayed here, signed with Sub Pop."

"Are they still together?"

"No, they broke up last year, and I don't know what he's been doing since."

"Sexual assaults, apparently."

Pete crosses to Scott's Mr. Coffee and pours himself a cup. He sips, recoils at the taste. "What's up with the coffee?"

"Jack Daniel's. I was working late a few nights ago and I added some Jack and the aftertaste hasn't quite gone away."

Pete tastes it again and doesn't mind it now. He looks for a place to sit, but a sawed-off shotgun and two bags of evidence, probably drugs, occupy the chair.

"Who's the victim," Scott asks.

"Amber Nickerson."

"Amber? Classic victim name. Who is she?"

"Girl who's new to the scene. She's friends with some guys in bands. I don't know much about her."

"How old?"

"Eighteen."

"Good looking?"

"I don't know."

Scott checks the cover sheet of the police report. "Five-foot seven, hundred and ten. Wonder if she prefers heroin or meth?"

"I'm leaving early today. I'll talk to you about this tomorrow."

"This should be a fun one to try."

"No. The plan is to get high bail so he stays in custody, and then we work out a plea."

"So what do you need me for?"

"Moral support."

New Kid In Town

AS SOON as Pete steps out of the courthouse he looks up at the sky. The nimbus clouds are breaking and there are patches of blue, but Pete expects rain. He believes it rains more in Seattle now than when he was growing up, though unlike local environmentalists he does not attribute this to the millennial decline.

He buttons his Burberry and walks north toward McCormick and Schmicks, picking up *The Stranger* at Buzzard Discs along the way.

The hostess knows Pete and seats him at his usual table in the southeast corner of the barroom, from where he can watch the street traffic. His waitress is attractive simply by virtue of her youthful features and smooth skin. She wears the standard black skirt and white blouse, but also purple tights.

"Haven't seen you here before," he says.

"I try not to work too much."

"Good plan."

He orders a Pyramid Pale Ale with a lemon, a dozen Quilcene yearling oysters on the half shell, and a bowl of white clam chowder.

"By the way, I'm Gina."

"Pete."

"You're going to like the oysters," Gina says, smiling, maybe flirtatiously. "Be back soon."

Opening *The Stranger,* he skims Dan Savage's column, learns a little about genital piercing, then turns to "I Saw U."

BUS STOP GIRL
near SAM, 3/10, with books and backpack. Me: in back of bus, hoping you would get on. You smiled at me when bus pulled away?

SUPERSUCKERS AT CROCODILE
Me: blond, glasses, front center stage. You: near sound booth, bowling shirt. Looking at me? I'm better to touch. Call if you want.

Pete guesses from the bowling-shirt reference that she saw John Schilling, who road-manages local bands. Pete wonders why she did not see *him.* He's taller than Schilling.

Through the course of lunch Pete has three Pyramids, and then a scotch and a Camel for dessert. There is a rule prohibiting county employees from drinking alcohol during work hours, but Pete considers himself finished for the day. Having nothing he has to do usually makes Pete edgy, but today he enjoys the afternoon's buzz and wonders about Gina.

"How long's your shift," he asks her as he hands over his Mastercard, downplaying the question as idle curiosity.

"I *thought* so," she says, checking out his credit card.

"What?"

"You're Pete Tyler." She looks back up at him. "My big sister turned me on to your first CD."

"Only CD," he says, now understanding the flirtation.

"She's going to be *so* jealous when she finds out I waited on you." Before Pete can think of anything to say, she asks, "Why are you wearing a suit?"

"Long story."

Gina nods. "I'll be right back."

Outside streetlights fizz on with an orangy glow and the sidewalk begins to fill with the nine-to-fivers. Pete watches the men in Brooks Brothers suits and wingtips and recalls when he was in the band and he would be dragging to breakfast at Denny's about this time of day, feeling sorry for people like that.

Now he is one of them and does not mind. He thinks the suit and wingtips look good on him, and he likes being able to afford a good lunch at a place where a pretty waitress will flirt with him, and he likes being lucid, or at least semi-lucid.

"My shift's over," she announces when she returns with his credit card and receipt.

A Farewell to Farms

GINA'S APARTMENT is a small studio on First Hill with pinewood floors and a bay window looking out on south downtown. Decorating style is liberal arts collegiate, including a black-and-white poster of Kurt Cobain playing an acoustic guitar.

Pete drinks a Rainier and sits on the couch and clicks on the TV with the remote, surfs between channels four, five, and seven, checking for Keith Junior's arraignment, but *Rosie O'Donnell, Oprah,* and *Inside Edition* are still on.

They took a taxi here because Gina wanted to change clothes, but she returns from the bathroom in the same outfit. Pete takes this as a good sign. He does not see any reason to leave.

No sense in giving up gained ground.

"Sorry the couch isn't more comfortable," she says, sitting down next to him, kicking her feet out onto the coffee table, skirt falling back a bit. *The Rocket* lies open on the table, folded to Johnny Renton's "Lip Service" gossip column. "My sister would *die* if she knew you were here." She guzzles her beer. "I'd call and tell her, but I'm not speaking to her. She still lives in Boise and she's married now and has a kid and a farm and everything, and she's kind of jealous of me. I moved to Seattle and all, and she didn't . . ."

Pete lights a Camel and while she talks about her sister he

checks out her legs—a couple inches of flesh is exposed between her purple thigh-highs and skirt.

"And," Gina continues, "she also hated the fact that I could faith-heal and she couldn't."

He looks up. *Faith-heal?* She either has an off-center sense of humor or *she's out of her teeny mind.*

"I can't do it anymore," Gina explains. "Our father was a minister. A real Holy Roller. And he said I had the gift." She shrugs. "But I lost it when I became a teenager because I lost the faith. I moved to Seattle and started doing drugs and drinking and everything else." She smiles. "The things you do when you lose God. Right?"

Pete stares at her. In the 1980s Seattle was a place people fled from, but in the 1990s it became a place people fled to—hundreds of young troubled souls moved here after Nirvana broke out and Pete wonders how he has somehow managed to meet most of them.

"Anyways," she continues, "I've lost it. Gone."

"Hold on just a minute."

Pete turns up the TV as a bizarre antidrug commercial comes on—something about your brain is an egg and the frying pan is heroin and all your friends are broken dishes—and it makes him want to stick a needle in his arm.

This is followed by anchorwoman Kathi Goertzen, who reports that "grunge musician Keith Johnson has been charged with raping a young woman from the local music scene." Pete flashes on Kathi G. in the Bad Old Days at the Watertown Tavern. A clip of Keith playing at Lollapalooza rolls for a few seconds, then recedes to a small corner image as his arraignment fills the rest of the screen.

"Keith must have really pissed that girl off," Gina says. "For her to report it like that."

Pete clicks off the TV when Dan Lewis segues to a story about local Navy fliers involved in the NATO bombing of Belgrade.

"Do you like Flop?" Gina asks as she gets up. "They were your era, weren't they?"

Flop was an excellent 1990s Seattle band whose career arc was portentously built into their name.

"No, actually they were a little later," he says. "We were more the era of Pure Joy, Rusty's previous band."

Pete watches as she bends over to put the CD into a boom box and his desire for her is in no way lessened by the crazy talk or the Keith Junior distraction.

"This place is too small," she says when she sits back down. "I'm moving next month."

"Bigger place?"

"House. I'm moving to Bellevue. *Yuck*." She finishes her beer. "I'm getting married. Want another Rainier?"

"I'm fine," he says, checking her left hand, confirming that she is not wearing a ring.

"I don't wear my ring when I'm working," she explains, following his eyes. "Bigger tips if I don't."

"Actually, I think I will have another beer."

While she makes a quick trip to the refrigerator, Pete wonders if there is still a possibility here.

"Do you believe in fate?" Gina asks as she sits down, a little closer this time.

Pete hates questions like this.

"I think it was fate I met you," she says. "I've been nervous about this marriage thing, and the fact I asked you back here indicates I *should* be nervous. Right?"

Pete opens the fresh beer, knows enough to stay quiet.

"I mean I've been thinking about, well, having sex with you, and I shouldn't be, should I?"

She puts the bottle to her mouth and Pete admires her mouth and thinks an obvious thought.

"Maybe fate introduced us," she says, after taking a long drink, "so I could face temptation like this."

Should you try to talk her into something she may regret for the rest of her life? Maybe hate you for? Maybe even want revenge for?

"Maybe," he says.

"Want to hear how I met him?"

No. "Sure."

"Well, about six months ago he came by for lunch one day and I didn't really notice him until he left a big tip. Then he came back a couple of days later, and I talked with him and he was kind of charming, in a stumbling kind of way, and I started thinking maybe I should let him know I was available. But without being too forward, without acting like a panting slut, you know . . ."

Pete lights a Camel, is left behind on the word *slut.*

". . . So anyways, it all happened really, really fast and I'm thinking, Oh my God, I'm supposed to be with this guy the rest of my life, and I don't know, you know?"

Pete nods. "I know." He puts out his cigarette in his empty beer bottle, reminds himself he's trying to quit.

She leans in toward him slightly, lips parted, eyes locking with his. Pete, for a heartbeat of a moment, considers making his exit before it's too late, but decides to kiss her while he's thinking it over. She responds by throwing her arms around his neck and opening her mouth and wiping her tongue across his front teeth.

His free hand reflexively moves under her skirt and up her bare leg, lightly sliding up her thigh with just his fingertips and then he palms the roundness of her ass and her skin is soft and smooth and he's once again reminded of how wonderful women's bodies are—*but she's engaged and half-crazy and this is a bad, bad, bad idea.*

But her hand goes to his groin, and that's that.

See You in the Next Millennium

PETE IS awakened by the bluish predawn light flooding through the bay window. He quietly slides out of bed, begins dressing.

"Good morning," Gina says, startling him.

"Good morning," he says. "I've got to get home before I go to the office."

"Oh."

"Sorry to wake you." He kisses her on the cheek. "Go back to sleep."

"What are you doing this weekend?"

Penance? "I'm not sure."

"Wanna go to the film festival?"

"Actually, I'm busy Friday. And Saturday I'm seeing the Fastbacks at the Crocodile." Pause. "I could put you on the guest list."

"Don't you have to be twenty-one to get in there? Or at least eighteen?"

Smoke

PETE FINDS Scott in the morning just outside the courthouse on Third Avenue, smoking near a coffee cart. No smoking is allowed in the building, so lawyers, judges, police, jurors, and defendants all mingle out here. Pete lights one of his Camels as he joins Scott. The clouds are low and dark but it is not raining yet.

"What was bail set at?"

"Fifty thousand. Judge wimped out. C.J. posted bail for him that night."

"Did you look over the police reports?"

Scott nods. "Sounds like a routine rock-and-roll night."

"How strong do you think the case is?"

"It's 'He said, she said.' But we've got him in two lies, including the big one where he first says they didn't have intercourse, then admits they did on tape. And the bit about not being able to find a condom when there were *three fucking dozen* lying all around the apartment?

"We win it if she's believable on the stand. We've got the torn underwear, the bruises on her legs, the bruising by his eye, and we can probably get his DNA from under her nails."

This matches Pete's appraisal. He nods.

Scott drops his cigarette and stomps it out. "And I like how he pretends he doesn't know who Tuiaia is talking about at first, then pauses when asked if she went back to his house with him, then asks if he needs a lawyer."

"We'll never get the lawyer thing in front of a jury."

"Maybe in this context?"

Pete shakes his head. " 'Insolubly ambiguous.' And the appellate unit is tired of arguing 'harmless error' on our appeals."

"Yeah, yeah, yeah, but we can slip in the ten-second pause."

"Depends on our judge."

Scott glances around. "Let's talk some more about suppressed evidence, just in case there are some jurors out here we can taint."

Pete laughs. "Anyway, we'll plead it out."

"Why?"

"Think about it. On the relative scale of things, this is not that egregious."

"I know, I know, but for the grace of God . . ." Scott lights up another Lucky Strike with his Zippo. "Are you going to take some grief from your old gang of ne'er-do-wells?"

Pete nods.

"You know," Scott says, "this case could make us sort of famous for a while."

"Only if it goes to trial."

"We could force it to trial. Offer nothing."

Pete shakes his head.

"Come on," Scott says. "We could have a good time with this. A little grief is a small price to pay for getting our mugs on TV."

"It won't be just a little grief. Seattle's still a small town."

"What? Do you actually *care* about that?"

"Before we do anything, we should set up an interview with the victim."

Meeting crime victims often affirms Pete's belief that his role as a prosecutor is right and good and meaningful, except when they change their stories and he wants to punch them.

Going to Bakeries

PETE COMES home late Friday evening and tosses his Burberry and his suit jacket on the hammock, dries his hair with a kitchen towel.

The emptiness of his loft usually appeals to him as it represents a commitment to minimal possessions, an ability to pack everything he owns into his vehicle and sail for a new port on a whim, even though he has no intention of indulging such a whim. At other times, such as when he's drunk, the emptiness strikes him as a metaphor for his life.

He pulls a beer out of the refrigerator, twists it open. He flicks the cap with a snap of his forefinger and thumb and it flies across the room like a mini Frisbee, ricochets off the wall near the clock.

Tonight's Resurrection Jukebox will have a theme: *the most depressing songs of all time.*

The first call is easy. He puts on Jonathan Richman and the Modern Lovers, circa 1976, first album, eighth track, "Hospital."

"*When you get out of the hospital, let me back into your life . . .*" The song begins like a funeral dirge, and it's downbeat from there. "*I go to bakeries all day long, there's a lack of sweetness in my life . . .*"

Toward the end, he decides to page Winter. He punches in his number, then calls back a moment later and leaves a voice mail in case she does not have her pager.

He follows Jonathan Richman with the Brains, "Money Changes Everything," circa 1982. "*She said sorry, baby, I'm leaving you tonight . . .*" This song scores extra points on the depression-irony scale as it received almost no airplay until covered by Cyndi Lauper.

Next up, "This Is the Day," from the The's *Soul Mining* album, circa 1983. "*You watch a plane fly across the clear blue sky, this is the day your life will surely change . . .*"

He considers following this with U2—"*nothing changes on New Year's Day*"—circa 1983, but there is something too intrinsically upbeat about U2. Also contemplated is the Cure's "How Beautiful You Are," circa 1987, "Los Angeles," by X, circa 1980, and even the Bangles' "Dover Beach," circa 1984, but Pete decides the eighties are overrepresented tonight. From the seventies there's "Behind Blue Eyes" or "How Many Friends" by the Who, circa 1971 and '75, but he finally digs out an old 45, "The Worst That Could Happen" by the Brooklyn Bridge, circa 1969. This is not a depressing song on its face, but it has always been a reliable downer for Pete.

The needle hits the vinyl of the 45 and there are pops and scratches and the singer's voice warbles a bit because of the slight warping of the disc. "*Maybe it's the best thing for you, but it's the worst thing that could happen to me. I'll never get married . . .*" The song fades out after a thundering crescendo of wedding-theme horns.

Tonight's wallow should climax here, but after another couple Rainiers, and no return call from Winter, Pete is spinning to new depths. He cues up Joy Division, circa 1979, "Love Will Tear Us Apart." "*Seeking different roads, love, love will tear it apart, again . . .*"

This calls to mind Beth, and the show where they met in Portland. Through a typical scheduling tragedy, Pete's band was on a bill with Christian Death and Tones on Tail, so-called death-rock groups, and it was a goth crowd.

Pete's band opened with a gleefully punk cover of Neil Diamond's "Solitary Man," which confused the audience. They then segued into their originals, noisy but melodic pop with a heavy bass line and cryptic lyrics. Vibes in the room progressed from confused to indifferent. For their own amusement, they finished with an especially gloomy version of the D.I.'s "Richard Hung Himself," which went over surprisingly well. They walked off to applause and spent the rest of the night backstage getting wrecked.

After shows, Pete would sometimes go out to the mosh pit area and look for things people had lost. He found earrings, watches, pearls, money, drugs, all sorts of miscellany. He did not find anything after this one, but he did see Beth, who had either hid from the security thugs or charmed them.

She wore lace-up boots and a black leather coat over a black tank dress. Her hair was dyed bluish-black, contrasting with her pale skin. Crosses hung from her pierced ears. She had left home a few days ago and was passing through on her way to Los Angeles and was hoping to sleep in the club, expecting it to be warmer and roomier than her VW Karmann Ghia.

This was the last gig of the tour, and the band was heading back to Seattle that night, so Pete stayed behind with Beth and rented a room in a downtown Portland hotel. The night clerk made Pete pay up front.

Their room was small and dingy with brown carpet. They both cringed when he turned on the light, so he clicked it off. They sat on the bed near the open window and shared a half rack of Mickey's Big Mouth and a pack of Camels.

Within two hours of meeting her, Pete knew more about Beth's family than he knew about his own. Abusive father, neurotic mother, trailer-park shenanigans—not unlike a lot of the stories he heard from girls he met on the road, but Beth impressed him with the way she had survived relatively undamaged. Also, she was willing to risk displaying her vulnerabilities, and she fell in love quickly and completely. This awed him. He always had a weakness for girls like her, before and after. Especially after.

He did not plan to have sex with her, at least not the first night. They undressed for bed as though they were simply friends sharing a room, though he watched her undress in his peripheral vision and noticed the split-heart tattoo on her ankle and the Egyptian eye—"Eye of Horus"—on the small of her back. They climbed into the stiff clean sheets on separate sides of the double bed, he in large white boxer shorts, she in frayed white panties.

Then she suddenly slid over and put her head on his shoulder. After a moment, he wrapped his arm around her. She snuggled her head further onto his chest. He wondered if she could hear his heart, which was beating fast. Then she kissed a rib and he felt it in his spine and he could not figure out why it felt so intense, but had the good sense not to wonder about this too much. He leaned over and kissed her forehead, and then kissed it again, longer, and then she turned her face up to him and he kissed her lips and it was a kiss that felt like it mattered.

He had an overwhelming urge to touch every part of her body and he started by breaking off the kiss and kneeling back and putting his hands lightly on her neck and then sliding them slowly down her chest, over her breasts, across her stomach, both hands moving toward her navel, and then he lightened his touch and glided his hands over the ends of her pubic hairs to the inside of her thighs and all the way down her legs to her ankles and feet and toes. He then kissed his way back up her body, which was goose-pimpled and twitching with small spasms.

She did not seem to have much sexual experience, surprisingly to Pete, but she followed his lead, her hands eventually duplicating the actions of his own, touching him in the same curious teasing way he touched her. This went on and on and on until they were both a mess of totally exposed desires.

The next day they drove out to Cannon Beach and checked into a motel with weekly rates and a kitchen. They stocked the refrigerator with orange juice, tequila, and two cases of Mickey's. The walls were white and blue with cheap prints of driftwood and stormy seas. During the day they walked the beach and talked about the past and present, but not the future.

At night they ate rolls and cold cuts with lots of mustard and then drank and had sex. The Cure, Joy Division, Tears for Fears, Love and Rockets, Talking Heads, the Psychedelic Furs, and the Smiths rotated on the cassette boom box. They played house from March until May, when the summer rates began and Pete ran out of money.

"There's a taste in my mouth as desperation takes hold . . ." The closing lyrics of the song snap him out of it. His eyes are oddly blurry and he decides to chase the Rainier with a scotch. Most of the liquor he pours makes it into the glass. The rest he figures will evaporate.

One of the things that gets him about Beth is that they never saw each other again. When they parted, they promised to write. She kept her promise.

Her first letter arrived at his parents' house, where he was temporarily staying. He felt a twinge of envy that she had left the Northwest for something new. He was bothered by a slew of grammatical errors, and by the fact that she was not as enthusiastically affectionate in print as she was in person. Still, he read the letter over and over and appreciated that it was signed, "Love Always."

He wrote back and asked her to send him a phone number as soon as she settled in somewhere. A couple weeks later, she did. His mother erased the message, so he did not get to hear her voice, but she saved the number. They traded phone calls for another week. When he finally reached her one late night, he could hear music and chatter in the background. Their conversation was repeatedly interrupted and lacked something.

By this time, Pete had started seeing Jayne, a Canadian model from Vancouver, B.C., he met at the Watertown. He was anxious to be away from his parents' house, so he spent a lot of time in B.C. Beth, he presumed, was meeting new people, including boys in bands. They both tried calling that summer, but only a couple times, and they did not connect.

Sometime in the fall he moved out of his parents' place, after Todd and Bob found a suitable rental house. He called Beth to give her the new number, but she had moved, and her roommate did not know to where, or would not tell him. Sometime around Christmas Beth left a message on his parents' answering machine, but he was with Jayne the Canadian by that time and did not call her back. This is one of the Top Ten Regrets of his life.

Suddenly he decides he must find Beth's letter. Clutching the bottle of Johnnie, he goes to the walk-in closet and pulls out a milk crate stuffed with letters and postcards from the past twenty years.

There is no method to the madness as he begins pulling out envelopes and tossing them to the side. He is not absolutely sure he saved it, but why wouldn't he? He has always been nostalgic, as evidenced by the hundreds of letters he is burrowing through. Old friends' names flash by, and there is the temptation to read more than a few, but he resists. Though a few extra minutes should not matter in finding a thirteen-year-old letter, time suddenly seems critical.

Soon as he sees it he knows it—he recognizes the loopy writing. He sets down the bottle and opens the weathered envelope.

DEAREST PETE,

HOW'S LIFE? MINES LESS FUCKED UP THAN IT COULD BE I GUESS. I'M STAYING WITH THESE GIRLS NAMED PLEASANT AND JENNIFER, WHO EVERYBODY CALS "FER"!! SHE'S CRAZIER THAN I AM AND DOES A LOT OF SPEED AND WONT SHUT UP, BUT SHE'S GOT A GOOD SOUL. SHE'S HEARD OF YOUR BAND. I TRY TO TELL HER ABOUT YOU, BUT IT'S HARD. PLEASANT AND JENNIFER LET PEOPLE STAY HERE IF THEY CHIP IN RENT. BELINDA CARLISLE USED TO LIVE HERE! EVERYONE CALLS THE HOUSE, "DISGRACELAND," IN HONOR OF GRACELAND.

She writes about some of the things they did together and some things Pete remembers, but some he had forgotten, and these hit him like finding a long-lost precious possession.

WHEN I STARTED THIS LETTER I WAS GOING TO WRITE SOME MUSHY STUFF BECAUSE I WAS FEELING SENTIMENTAL BUT IT'S HARD, YOU

KNOW. I DON'T KNOW HOW YOU WRITE LIKE YOU DO. I THINK IT'S
MUCH HARDER TO WRITE THINGS THAN TO SAY THEM BECAUSE I
DON'T KNOW HOW YOUR REACTING. ARE YOU AND THE GUYS STILL
THINKING BOUT COMING HERE TO L.A.?

She goes on to tell Pete things about L.A. he would find out on
his own when the band came there two years later. He hoped she
might just show up at one of the shows, or he would see her at
a club like the Rainbow or the Whiskey or Madame Wong's, but
it did not happen.

Later he heard she had become a stripper and had moved to
Portland. There were rumors that she was seen in Portland or
Los Angeles or Seattle, but Pete never saw her.

On the kitchen table he opens his IBM laptop—the same
model Judge Ito promoted during the O.J. trial. He plugs in a
phone cord and logs onto the Microsoft Network. Using the
MSN Person Finder, he looks up Beth Keller.

Pleased to Meet Me

PETE BELIEVES he is almost not drunk. He waits impatiently as the metal garage door slides up, then swings the blue 1980 Volvo out onto Western, south toward Madison. The Jesus and Mary Chain's "Psychocandy" plays through a Blaupunkt stereo and ADS speakers, which cost more than the Volvo is currently worth.

Capitol Hill seems a likely place for Beth to live, so Pete trusts the address on Boylston Place for B. Keller must be hers. He passes Dick's, notices the police cruisers in the parking lot and flashes on the days when he would have been subject to their suspicion.

Near Cornish College of Arts he locates the apartment building, The Hanging Gardens, which is a U-shaped double-story structure with ivy climbing the bricks of the units that face an open courtyard—just the type of place Beth would like. No parking anywhere, as usual on Capitol Hill, so Pete double-parks and clicks on his hazards.

He walks the concrete pathway past the fountain where a chipped concrete dolphin with water spouting from its mouth is perched in the middle of a round pool glowing blue. Beth liked water. She even liked the bad ocean artwork on the wall of their motel room.

There appear to be four apartments in each wing of the building, two upstairs and two down. Pete checks the mailbox of the middle wing and there it is: KELLER, 2B.

Suddenly he wonders what the hell he's doing? What will she look like? What will she say? What will *he* say?

It's been a while, but you were always the best and . . .

He decides he is better off not thinking about this and simply marches up the stairs. He stops at the door marked 2B—*2B or not 2B . . .* He listens. Nothing. He knocks.

Sounds come from within. Pete feels the surge of nervousness, but it's not an unpleasant buzz.

The peephole shows light, then turns dark. A moment later the door opens and a twenty-something guy with a goatee is standing there.

New boyfriend?

"What?" the guy says.

"Is Beth home?"

Pete is suddenly conscious of his clothes—he is still wearing a blue suit, though without tie.

"She moved," the goatee guy says.

"How long ago?"

"Last month."

"Do you know where she went?"

"No. Dancing somewhere, I suppose."

Stripping.

"Who are you?" the guy finally asks.

"I'm an old friend of hers."

The guy nods. "She has a lot of old friends."

"Do you know if she's coming back?"

"Yeah, but not to here."

"Do you know how I can get a hold of her?"

The guy shakes his head. "She moves around a lot."

"Can I leave you my name and number, just in case she checks in?"

"Sure. Whatever."

Pete starts to give him one of his deputy prosecutor cards, then thinks better of this. "Do you have a pen?"

The guy looks put out, but walks off and returns with a pencil. Pete writes his name and number on a matchbook from the Romper Room.

Gotcha Outside the Cha Cha

EXHAUSTION MIXED WITH mild depression catches up to Pete as he drives back down Broadway. He turns on the Cure, "In Between Days," track 15 of the singles collection. *"Yesterday I got so old I felt like I could die . . ."*

There would be no way to know from the attire of the kids walking the sidewalks that the Cure entered the scene in 1976, that *Never Mind the Bollocks, Here's the Sex Pistols* came out in 1977, that the Fastbacks formed in 1979, *twenty years ago.*

Pete notices a particularly punkish couple: skinny guy with ripped Levi's and Flock of Seagulls haircut, his arm wrapped around a waifish girl with ripped Levi's and blue hair. Pete wonders what bands they're talking about? He would love to be that age again and talking with a blue-haired girl about Nick Cave or Ziggy Stardust or anybody.

As he drives past Bimbo's Bitchin Burrito Kitchen he slows down and cranes his neck to see how things look inside. He remembers a dark-haired cool girl from the band Carissa's Weird who served him last time he was there. He did not ask for her phone number and later wished he had. She would not likely date a prosecutor, but might get drunk with the former singer of Morph.

Suddenly wig-wag lights flash behind him. Pete pulls over for the officer to pass. The officer, however, pulls directly behind Pete.

Fuck me.

Pete turns off the stereo and puts his early career experience prosecuting vehicular assaults and DUIs to good use by quickly adding up his alcohol intake: three or four beers at lunch, one scotch. Another three beers at home? And another three or four ounces of scotch? About twelve ounces total, but the burn-off is about .015 per hour, and Pete was drinking for about seven hours, which puts him between .11 and .13?

Career-ending stupidity is what he figures it adds up to as the officer approaches his window. He always knew his professional ruin would be due to a woman, but is surprised it has come from one he has not seen in years.

"License and registration please."

Pete's deputy prosecutor I.D. is, fortunately, close to his driver's license. Unfortunately, he spastically mishandles his wallet.

He can already picture the police report: *Defendant fumbled drunkenly for license.*

"Pete Tyler?" The officer looks familiar. Was he a witness on a case? The I.D. badge says TOMARAS.

"Hey," Pete says, "how you doing?"

"Good. How are *you* doing? You were weaving all over the road."

"Oh, I was just looking to see if this girl I know was waitressing over there."

Pete gestures at Bimbo's. Tomaras follows his gaze. Pete takes the opportunity to carefully pull his license out of his wallet.

"I don't need to see your I.D."

Pete sets his license and wallet on the passenger seat to avoid any more dexterity tests.

"Have you been drinking much?"

Pete stares back, glassy-eyed no doubt. There are only two smart things to do when an officer asks an incriminating question: tell the truth or say nothing.

"What?" Pete says.

"How much have you had to drink?"

Pete says slowly, "I'm not exactly sure."

Tomaras is checking him out and Pete knows that the officer is seeing all the signs he sees with people over the legal limit.

"Why don't you pull forward into that parking spot and get out of the vehicle."

Pete carefully puts the Volvo in gear, inches over, pulls on the emergency brake. He watches his balance as he steps out.

Tomaras uses the radio in his cruiser. Pete waits, lights a cigarette. He wishes he was not sweating because he knows it reeks of intoxicants.

Suddenly Kim Warnick appears out of the Cha Cha Lounge, which adjoins Bimbo's. She waves and yells, "Pete! Come on in! I'm bartending!" She's wearing a black Ramones T-shirt.

Tomaras steps out of his car.

"Hey!" Kim yells at the officer. "Don't give him a ticket!"

"Give me five minutes," Pete says to Kim, surprisingly unslurred.

Kim shrugs, steps back inside.

Tomaras puts his hand on Pete's shoulder, nearly causing Pete to lose his balance. "Why don't you go over there." He points at Kim, who is now pressing her face up against the round Cha Cha window. "And have some coffee."

Pete takes a moment to appreciate the officer's apparent understanding of contradictory human impulses.

"Do you get what I'm saying?"

"Thanks."

Kiss of Beth

"DOUBLE SCOTCH for you," Kim yells when he enters. The Cha Cha is a cross between a Mexican resort and a punk club. Kim is behind the bar, a tropical hut in the middle of a poorly lit space. She holds out a tall glass for Pete. He accepts and takes a long drink. The Pixies' "Debaser" blasts from multiple speakers.

"Hey, Pete!" Andrew from Shuggie signals him with a cocktail held high. Andrew is married to a prosecutor, but tonight he is out with Sam from Love As Laughter, and Mike, a drummer from more bands than Pete can remember, and Danielle, the prettiest stripper at the Lusty, a tall true blonde.

Pete joins them, slipping in next to Danielle.

"Did he write you a citation or anything?" Andrew asks.

Pete shakes his head, lights a Camel.

"Favoritism," Danielle says. She puts a Marlboro Light to her frosted red lips and Pete picks up her Bic lighter from the table and clicks it on. She holds his hand as he lights her cigarette.

"So tell us what's up with Keith Junior," Sam says.

"I can't really tell you anything at this point."

"There's no way he raped that girl," Mike says.

"*You* don't know," Danielle says to Mike.

"I heard she spent the night with him and then claimed she'd been raped a day later."

Danielle turns to Pete. "Is that what happened?"

"I really can't say anything at this point."

"What's *that* mean?" Andrew says. "Don't go turning fucking *official* on us."

"Keith *is* a drunk and a drug addict and a fuck-up," Mike notes. "But not a rapist. He's not that ambitious."

Pete gestures for Kim to join them, hoping to change the subject, then he turns to Danielle, who looks suddenly glum. "Have you heard anything about Beth being in town?" he asks her.

She shakes her head.

"Beth?" Kim says, sliding into the booth next to Pete, who has to slide over farther toward Danielle. "Did I hear you say *Beth?*"

Pete nods, moves the ashtray between himself and Danielle.

"Beth," Kim repeats, "what can I do?" She slides out and hurries back to the bar.

"So how have you been?" Pete says to Danielle.

Danielle shrugs. "Depressed."

"Any particular reason?"

"The clouds. Ninety-three goddam record-setting days of rain this winter, or whatever it was. The same old same old. I don't know."

"You still with what's-his-name?"

What's-his-name is an incumbent who does not know how good he has it and puts Pete in mind of the Joe Jackson song, "Is She Really Going Out with Him?"

"Off and on." Danielle shrugs. "On right now. He's been okay lately."

Suddenly the Pixies are cut off the stereo and the room is weirdly quiet. Pete looks over at Kim, who is hunched over the CD player.

The piano intro of "Beth," the Kiss classic, fades in and Kim turns it up. "*Beth, I hear you callin'* . . ."

Pete laughs, as does everyone at the table.

Kim walks back to the booth, holding a scotch bottle to her mouth, singing along. Andrew joins in—"*Me and the boys are playing and we just can't find the sound"*—and Kim fills Pete's glass with scotch and he takes a drink and then starts singing along with Andrew and Kim—*"Oh, Beth, what can I do?"*— and others in the bar join in and it becomes a drunken sing-along, and mostly on-key, thanks to the slew of band members in the room, several of whom are with unsigned bands listed at seattlesounds.com.

The Idea

A PIERCING ache wakes Pete at about five A.M. His head is shrieking with the kind of pain that makes you promise to God you will never drink alcohol again if only He will help you survive last night's mistakes and regret.

But God helps those who help themselves, and Pete recognizes that he must *do* something, though he's in no condition to do anything, other than maybe vomit.

Blue predawn light blazes through the windows and threatens to turn Pete into dust. He forgot to shut the blinds, of course. He is surprised to see that at least he got his clothes off.

He sits up and suddenly it's total George Lucas THX Surround-Sound pain. He clumsily untangles himself from the sheets and plants his feet on the floor. He breathes heavily in anticipation of the next effort: standing.

Everything goes purple and yellow when he advances to a simian crouch. He decides to crawl, strategizing that he will be better off if he keeps his head low to the floor.

Granules of dirt press into Pete's knees. He trudges on to the refrigerator and reaches up for a bottle of water. He sucks the liquid down and the cold clear water seems to be just what he needs. Suddenly, though, the cold is too cold and his head starts shrieking. He drops the bottle.

Codeine is in the bathroom. *So close and yet so far away.* Calculating that crawling would take too long, he puts his hand on the kitchen counter island and pulls himself to his feet.

His feet, *God bless them,* carry him to the bathroom, where he finds the bottle of 222's, codeine aspirin from Canada. He gobbles down four. Vision clearing, he spots an old bottle of Vicodin.

Vicodin, same opiate family as codeine?

Vitamin bottles topple as he gropes for the prescription bottle. He wrestles the childproof cap open, then crunches down on a large football-shaped pill.

The drug is bitter on his tongue, so he puts his head under the faucet for water. Here he notices that there are puke chunks in the sink. Presumably his own from last night, *hopefully* his own. At least he got to the sink.

He dimly remembers the Cha Cha and Kim pouring him multiple scotches and people asking questions about Keith Junior. Then somebody started a sing-along of "Beth," and he does not remember who, but suspects he may be to blame.

Back in bed, he waits motionless for the drugs to kick in. He watches clouds float in from the south over Elliott Bay, their shadows darkening the white-capped water.

Minutes pass and the blue light loses its edge and softens with gray.

Rain is coming, *the shamanic Seattle rain.*

Many times he has laid awake in the early A.M. and ideas have come to him that seemed brilliant, but then he falls back asleep and the next day the ideas are either forgotten or have lost their shine.

Pete is vaguely conscious of this pattern. Still, he welcomes these early A.M. ideas. Some of them he has actually acted upon, including the notions to start the band and go to law school and pursue an adult life. While the adult life still eludes him, the band and law school he chalks up as accomplishments.

Thunder cracks and Pete looks for the lightning but does not see any. Rain starts falling hard and the south wind drives the drops against the windows. There's a flash of lightning over the Olympic Mountains, a darkening of the sky, and another crack of thunder. He closes his eyes—which seems to amplify the elements—and another early A.M. idea comes to him.

Daughter

"PETE? PETE. *Pete!*"

Awakened by the answering machine, he fumbles for the cordless phone, which is on the floor next to the futon.

"Hello?" he mutters.

"Did I wake you?" Winter says.

Pete's throat hurts, his head feels dull, his stomach is upset—all the usual signs of life on a Saturday morning. Last night starts coming back to him in fuzzy images. He groans.

"I woke you."

"It's okay. What's up?"

"Pete, I'm just so pissed off." Sounds like she's been crying.

"What's wrong?"

"I just talked to my mom and she just pisses me off and I keep trying because I think someday it will be different but instead it's the same shit." She talks fast, out of breath. "She's always criticizing, but if you *dare* to criticize *her* she completely guilts you out. I don't even know what the hell we were fighting about today. It started with the usual shit about how I'm never going to attract a man if I keep dancing at a strip club—and she doesn't even get that it's *not* a strip club—and I remind her that she's never kept a boyfriend longer than a year and the ones she did have were psychos or perverts and I remind her of the one she had when I was twelve and the shit he did when she wasn't around and she started just *screaming* that I was trying to guilt her out, and things got crazy from there." Winter finally pauses. "Goddam, she just makes me fucking *furious* and I know I shouldn't care so much but . . ."

This goes on for a few minutes more and Pete says almost nothing, remembers *the idea*.

"Thanks for listening," Winter says when she finishes.

"Anytime."

"You don't think I'm a bad person or anything, do you?"

"Hey," he says, "you're the best."

"You're just saying that."

"Winter, if you ever need a kidney transplant, I'll give you one of mine."

Sister Knows Best

SENSELESS SCREAMING of children in the distance is the first thing Pete hears as he walks up to the front door of his sister Katie's house. Multicolored "Happy Birthday" balloons tied to the porch railing squeak against each other in the breeze, aggravating his lingering hangover.

"You're not as late as expected," Katie says when she opens the door.

He hands her a large package wrapped in brown paper grocery bags as he steps inside.

"Nice wrapping job," she says.

"It's a boom box. CD and cassette."

"He's *four*."

"I included a Mudhoney CD." He takes off his ragged Shetland sweater and hangs it on the coat rack. "*Every Good Boy Deserves Fudge*. A classic."

"If you ever have a child, I'm buying him a drum set," Katie says. "You want a drink?"

"No." Pause. "Well, okay."

Pete follows her down the hall. He can still hear kids, but does not see any sign of them. "Where are the little irritants?" he asks.

"In the game room downstairs."

His sister's house is in Medina, on the east side of Lake Washington near Bill Gates's monstrosity. "Eastside" was a word Pete and Katie used in high school to describe the especially white-bread and uncool. Still, here Katie is in a white Colonial on the lake with five bedrooms, a formal dining room, a large country kitchen, a game room with a pool table and video games, and her husband's den.

The den always reminds Pete of his father's, but his father's had more books and no computer equipment. The scotch supply, however, is roughly equivalent.

Katie pours Pete a glass of Laphroaig, neat, and one for herself, to which she adds an ice cube.

"Like God spitting in your mouth," Pete says, tasting it.

"At least Dad taught us to appreciate good scotch."

"Never mind the fact that it killed him."

"Well, here's to him."

They touch glasses. Pete sits in a forest-green leather chair near the fireplace. He looks out the paned window at the lake and the dock with the ski boat tied up.

Pete did not expect his little gen-X sister to ever live like this. In high school she was "alternative," dark hair dyed even darker, severe black eyeliner, black turtlenecks with black skirts and black leggings over long skinny legs. She was reading poets like Rimbaud, Blake, and Ginsberg before she had a driver's license. When he was a junior at Nathan Hale High School she started seventh grade at Jane Addams across the street and some of his friends said she was a geek, but Pete thought she was cool and defended her. She turned him on to several bands, including Sonic Youth, Violent Femmes, and one that inspired him to start his own: the Replacements, or, as she called them, the Mats.

After she graduated from Evergreen State College, she moved into an Eastlake house near the Zoo Tavern with four other recent graduates. She was hanging out with Xana La Fuente, who was the girlfriend of the singer for Mother Love Bone, Andy Woods. Woods died from a heroin overdose three months after the eighties ended.

At the wake for Woods, which was held in the Paramount

Theatre, Katie told Pete she thought it was "sexy" for a man to have a job. She said she now wanted a man in "a gray flannel suit," referring to Gregory Peck in the movie. Pete suspected she also meant someone like their father, a respected political figure and lawyer, his alcohol problem notwithstanding.

In her late twenties she took a job in graphic art design at Microsoft and met and married William, a top executive worth, Pete suspects, zillions. Pete does not know what exactly William's job involves, but William is obviously thrilled that a girl as cool as Katie would have him, and he treats her well, so Pete thinks he's okay. Also, Pete knows Microsoft is going to take over the world, and he is glad to have connections in the coming regime.

"Who's going to handle the Keith Junior case?"

"Me. And Scott Foss."

Katie nods. "I heard some things about him from a couple different girls. This kind of thing."

"Keith or Scott?"

She smiles. "Keith."

"I doubt it's a first for him."

"Alcohol and drugs involved?"

"Alcohol. I don't know about drugs."

"He probably invited her back to his place for something to drink, some drugs, music, the usual rap."

Pete nods. *Sounds familiar.*

"The way he was going," Katie says, "it was just a matter of time before something like this happened." She looks at him. "This is going to be intense for you, isn't it? Prosecuting a guy from the scene?"

He pulls himself out of the chair for another scotch. After pouring himself a couple ounces, he holds out the bottle of Laphroaig to Katie.

"Thanks," she says.

He pours her an ounce, stays standing, decides to put the idea out there: "I'm getting married."

Katie stares at him. "Oh my God."

"Exactly."

She smiles. "You're getting married?"

He nods.

"To whom? Winter?"

"No."

"Who?"

"I don't know yet."

"What?"

"I'm not sure who exactly I'm going to marry."

Katie's smile fades. "Do you have somebody in mind?"

"No."

"I thought you were getting more normal as you got older, but clearly not."

"Hey, I'm getting married. That's pretty normal."

"Most people have a particular person in mind."

"It's not that easy. I can't drop by Seven-Eleven and pick up a bride. 'Excuse me, I'd like something fresh faced, to go.' " Pete reaches for his Camels.

"I thought you were quitting."

"I am." He puts a cigarette in his mouth.

"Please try to keep the smoke outside."

He turns the window crank. A fresh breeze blows in smelling of cedar. He lights up, throws the match out the window.

"Pete?"

"Yes?"

"You are too alone—I think it's getting to you. You're probably the most alone person I've ever known."

Pete considers. "Are you counting Lori James's brother?"

"What are you saying? You're not as alone as a sixteen-year-old boy who committed suicide?"

"Wasn't suicide. It was autoerotic asphyxiation."

"You mean erotic autoasphyxiation?"

"I thought it was called autoerotic asphyxiation."

"No, I'm pretty sure it's erotic autoasphyxiation."

"Wouldn't autoerotic make more sense?"

"No, it's erotic auto, not autoerotic."

"What's the difference?"

"*Stop.* Did you say Lori's brother . . . did this?"

"Right."

"How do you know?"

"Lori told me."

"When?"

"One night when we were drinking at Golden Gardens. Senior year."

"Wow." Katie shakes her head. "I can't believe that never got around school."

"Lori told everybody he hung himself. She just left out the masturbation part."

"Girls always told you secrets," she says. "How did you get them to do that?"

"They wanted to."

"But you never told them anything, really."

"I've always told you things."

"I don't count. I'm your sister."

Pete knocks his ash out the window.

"So what inspired this?" she asks.

"What?"

"This marriage talk." She studies him for a moment. "Is this connected to Keith Junior?"

"I've just been thinking about the future lately, that's all."

Pete appreciates that his sister is big on introspection, but he does not recognize that this may account for how her life has evolved while his has, essentially, not. Leading an examined life has its advantages, but Pete likes to point out what happened to Oedipus when he asked too many questions.

"Do you think I should marry Beth?"

"Are you kidding?"

"I'm not sure."

"When did you start seeing her again?"

"I haven't."

"You haven't?"

"But I heard she's back in town."

"Pete," she says, "you're kidding me, right?"

"No."

"This doesn't sound well thought out."

"Sure it does. Just like I decided I was going to form a band. I had no idea what I was doing, but a few months later we were playing clubs and girls were writing their numbers on my hands. Then I decided I was going to go to law school. I had no idea what I was thinking, but a few years later I'm sending people to jail."

"This is a little different."

"And look at you. You suddenly decided you were tired of hanging out with losers, and *boom,* you're married and have this total grown-up life."

"There was more to it than that."

"Okay, I'm listening."

"Pete, when you meet the *one,* you'll be scared."

"Scared? Great."

"You'll be scared because you'll know she could be it," Katie says patiently. "And that will scare you."

"Rosie O'Donnell scares me—should I marry *her?*"

"I'm glad you're thinking about this, but you're not ready to get married. Not yet. First, you have to be open to the idea of totally loving someone and letting yourself be loved, which is a completely scary and crazy feeling."

"Hey, I'll try anything once."

"And you have to be ready to make the hellish sacrifices."

"Sacrifices? That I know something about."

"You *think* you do. But you don't. It sometimes means putting someone else's happiness ahead of your own, and that's especially hard for someone who's set in his ways."

"I'll tell you one thing that worries me."

"Okay."

"Once you have a spouse and children, you can't kill yourself in good conscience."

"Sure you can." Katie smiles. "You just have to kill them first."

"Okay, now this is helping."

"Let me tell you something encouraging. Seriously."

"That's kind of what I was looking for."

"It's a huge relief when you get involved with someone to the point where life is no longer just about yourself."

As Pete takes a contemplative drag of his cigarette, the door opens and in steps William. Pete freezes, *busted*.

"Hi, Pete. How's rock-and-roll prosecution?"

Pete is not sure if this is a reference to the Keith Junior case or routine banter. He moves the cigarette out the window.

"How are things downstairs?" Katie asks.

"The clown arrived and everyone went out back."

"Sorry I've been up here so long, but Pete's worried about his future."

"Did you hear that Arkansas is proud of Clinton?" William says to Pete. "All these women who had sex with him are coming forward—and none of them are his sister."

Pete smiles. "So, how's the Microsoft plan for world domination coming?"

"You know I can't talk about that." William always plays along dryly.

Katie takes William's hand and kisses him quickly on the lips and Pete is moved by this spontaneous gesture of bonding and affection.

Fears of a Clown

THE CLOWN in Katie's backyard is made up in the manner of Seattle legend J. P. Patches: ragged clothes, floppy shoes, multicolored porkpie hat, humongous mouth. J.P. was on local television through the sixties and seventies. What Pete remembers is that J.P. banged kitchen pans and had a sidekick named Gertrude, who was a man unconvincingly dressed as a woman—even a five-year-old could see Gertrude was a man wearing a mop as a wig.

What could be funnier?

Nearly every local grammar school kid of that time watched J.P. in the morning. However, J.P. was canceled about the time *Sesame Street* started, so the J.P. look is a reference point only for the parents.

The clown entertains the semicircle of children by pulling scarves out of a variety of orifices.

Pete's mother joins him on the edge of the gathering.

"Have you looked up Beth?" she asks.

"*What?*" he says, jolted.

"Weren't you going to look her up—Beth?"

Then he remembers their conversation. "Oh, right. No, no, not yet."

"Did you confirm a time for dinner with Winter?"

"I'm sorry, I forgot."

"Peter, I really would like to meet these women you date. Is that asking too much?"

"Do you know the name of the clown?"

"The name of the clown?"

"Yes."

"Bippo, I think."

"No, I mean the name of the man. Who is he? Do we have references?"

"References? For a *clown*?"

Pete wonders if the clown might be a pedophile. This is not the kind of thought Pete is glad to have come into his head and he wonders if maybe he has been in the Sexual Assault Unit too long.

"Forget it," he says.

"Katie has a good life here," his mother says, "doesn't she?"

"Yes. It's nice her husband is a zillionaire."

"That's not what I meant, Peter."

Pete stares at the clown, as though he actually cares how many colored scarves the poor bastard can pull out of his nose. The clown finishes the scarf trick by squeezing them into a ball, which he seemingly swallows. The children clap and squeal.

Katie crosses over. "Either of you want a drink from the house?" she asks.

"Do you have a business card for the clown?"

"Peter?" his mother says.

"Why?" Katie says.

"Do you know his name?"

"Bippo."

"No, the name of the man."

"Jimmy."

"*Jimmy?*"

"Why?"

"What do you know about him?"

"He's a clown?"

"Where did you hear about him?"

"The O'Conners hired him for their little girl's birthday."

"Get me his name," Pete says. "Full name. And date of birth if you can."

"*Why?*"

"So I can run a criminal check."

"Oh my God."

"I'm serious. Pedophiles love jobs like this."

"Don't creep me out."

"Sorry, it's a long shot. But get me his name."

Katie sighs. "Do you want a drink?"

"No thanks. I have to drive pretty soon."

"Don't you want to stick around for the molestation?"

"Would you two *stop*," their mother finally says, mostly to Pete. She turns to Katie. "I asked Peter if I could meet one of these women he's dating, so he's trying to change the subject. And I'll have another glass of the Merlot, thank you."

The clown, meanwhile, twists a balloon into the shape of a wiener dog. He then pets the wiener balloon, which results in high-pitched squeaks. This delights the five-year-olds, some of whom laugh and some of whom cover their ears and scream.

Pete and his hangover can stand no more. "Talk to you later, Mother." He points to his ears as an explanation for the early exit.

His hand goes for the Camels as he walks down the long lawn to the lake, but he stops himself because he is still within sight of his mother.

The yard stretches two hundred feet to the dock and the dock is another thirty feet and the sounds of the children mercifully fade as Pete focuses on the familiar sound of the water lapping against the pilings.

A green light in a brass ship fitting is fixed to the end of the dock. This is one of the reasons Katie wanted to buy the house. "Gatsby believed in the green light," Katie is fond of saying to Pete when she has been drinking. William, ever the practical one, pointed out that a fifty-dollar fixture should not be the deciding factor in a 5.8-million-dollar purchase.

Boats against the current, borne back ceaselessly into the past.

404 B

DETECTIVE TUIAIA enters and drops a police report on Pete's desk, then helps himself to the Starbucks.

Pete looks up. "I've already got too many open cases."

"This is just follow-up on Keith Johnson."

Pete reaches for the pages. Tuiaia sits.

"I appreciate the work here," Pete says when he finishes reading. "But we can't use it."

"Why not?"

"For starters, she's adamant she doesn't want to testify."

"You've talked witnesses into it before."

"Bradley, I know Danielle, and I'm not going to talk her into this. Particularly when I don't think the testimony is admissible anyway."

"He did basically the same thing to her."

"Basically, but it's not distinctive enough to call it an M.O. under 404 B. I'm not going to brief this and put her on the stand for a pretrial hearing—expose her like that—when I know there's not a judge in this building that will let that evidence go to the jury."

Tuiaia stares. "Where's the trademark zealousness? You're not going to let me down on this, are you?"

Sometimes in Winter

THEY ARE going at it on the floor near the stereo and Pete puts one hand under her ass and wraps the other hand around her naked back, which is slippery with sweat, then lifts her off the floor, rises to his knees, and, finally, stands, all the while staying inside her while Offspring's "Self Esteem" blasts.

She moves her hands to the top of his shoulders and grabs on crazily and gyrates, her red thigh-high stockings rubbing on his ribs as he tries to cross the room and stay inside her at the same time.

He makes it to the futon where he drops her down onto her back without losing the coupling and she moves her hands to his hips and pushes and pulls along with his body.

As the pace picks up, Winter starts screaming, "Fuck me, fuck me, *fuck me like we're in Tacoma . . .*"

Then things get dirty.

Five Years

WINTER WALKS to the refrigerator, naked except for the thigh-highs. She resembles Bettie Page with her black hair and bangs. She has a nose stud, a tongue stud, a navel stud, and multiple piercings in her right ear that put Pete in mind of fishing lures.

"Who's Gina?" she asks as she pulls a bottle of water out of the refrigerator.

"Who?" Pete is still on the futon, winded.

She takes a long drink, wipes water off her chin. "Gina. Her number is on the counter."

"Oh. Waitress."

"Did you fuck her?"

"Yeah."

"Still seeing her?"

"No. No. Definitely not."

Winter reaches into her lunchbox purse, which is on the floor next to where their sexual escapades started an hour or so ago. She pulls out cigarettes and a piece of paper.

Pete wipes the sweat off his face with a pillow. The sheets and down comforter are in a tousled heap at the foot of the futon.

Winter crosses over and sits down. She hands him the paper. "Wrote it at work today."

The page is filled with teeny handwriting, all capital letters, without any paragraphs or spacing.

BETTIE WAS NOT IN A GOOD MOOD TO START WITH. THINGS GOT WORSE WHEN HER MANAGER CHEWED HER OUT FOR "A LACK OF PUNCTUALNESS" AND TOLD HER SHE COULD NOT WORK TODAY BECAUSE SHE WAS LATE. BETTIE ASKED IF SHE COULD STAY LONG ENOUGH TO FINISH FILING HER NAILS BUT THE BITCH WOULD NOT EVEN GIVE HER THAT LITTLE PIECE OF DIGNITY. BETTIE SNAPPED. SHE STABBED THE MANAGER IN THE NECK WITH THE NAILFILE AND BLOOD SQUIRTED OUT AND IT REMINDED HER OF A MAN CUMMING BECAUSE EVERYTHING IN THE LUSTY REMINDED HER OF THAT. BETTIE WAS GLAD TO LEAVE, GLAD TO LEAVE BEHIND THE SMELL OF LYSOL AND CUM. SHE WALKED, DIDN'T RUN, TO PETE'S PLACE, AND ON THE WAY SHE NOTICED A SPOT OF BLOOD ON HER SHIRT AND THIS REMINDED HER OF A BOY FROM WHEN SHE WAS SIXTEEN. THEY WERE HANGING OUT ON THE ROCKS AT GOLDEN GARDENS WATCHING THE BOATS COME IN AND HE KISSED HER FOR THE FIRST TIME AND WHEN THEY STOPPED MAKING OUT SHE NOTICED SEVERAL SPOTS OF BLOOD ON HER LOLLAPALOOZA T-SHIRT. IT TOOK THEM A WHILE TO REALIZE THAT HE HAD CUT HIS HAND ON A ROCK AND EVERYWHERE HE TOUCHED HER HE LEFT A SPOT.

Pete looks up when he finishes. Winter is staring at him, playing with an unlit cigarette.

What to say? "I like it."

"I should probably change the names," she says, setting down the story, "in case my manager sees it." Bettie is Winter's stage name. "Someday I'm going to write a story about you, Pete."

"Yeah?"

"I'm thinking of taking a writing class."

"You should."

"You really think so?"

"Yes, I do."

"I have a lot of stories saved up."

"I know."

"You're the only person I've shown most of them to."

For the first time in the months they have been periodically seeing each other, he tries to imagine a life with Winter. Though this is not easy, neither is it impossible.

"Winter," he says, "what would you like to be doing in five years?"

"Something different."

"Different from what?"

"From what I'm doing now."

"Well, like what?"

"I'd like to have kids," she says. "But I'd like to get married first."

"I didn't realize you were so old-fashioned."

She smiles. "There's lots you don't know."

"I don't doubt it."

She finally lights the cigarette.

"Smoking menthols?" Pete frowns.

"Yeah, I thought it would help me quit, but instead it's like having dessert all the time."

He picks up an ashtray and a pack of Camels from the floor.

"Kids?" he says. "Why did you say you want to have kids?"

"I don't know," she says. "Five years is a long time. Remember that song 'Five Years' by Bowie? 'I thought I saw you in an ice cream parlor—' "

"—'Drinking milkshakes cold and long.' "

"I never knew what the fuck the song was about, but I loved it."

"It's about death and sex."

"You think *every*thing's about death and sex."

"Everything is."

Winter smiles, then takes a long drag of her menthol, exhales slowly. "I've been talking to people about the Keith Junior thing."

"Yeah?"

"A lot of his friends are really pissed. They think Amber shouldn't have gotten the police involved."

"Shouldn't have gotten the police involved in a rape?"

"Well, they think she's exaggerating."

"What do you think?"

"She put herself in a stupid situation—I'm not saying it wasn't fucked-up what he did, because it was. But still, sometimes when you put yourself in a shitty situation, shitty things are going to happen. Any girl around here knows when you're drinking it up with Keith . . . well, hey, anything goes. You know? Everyone knows that about him."

"She's eighteen."

"I know. I know who she is. I feel bad for her, I feel bad about the shit she's going to have to deal with, but the important thing is to deal with it, and I don't know if reporting it to the cops is going to make it any easier for her. I don't think a public spectacle is going to help anybody." She grinds her cigarette out. "I once wrote a story about rape. Never showed you that one."

"Are you going to?"

"I don't know. Probably not."

"I'd like to read it if you want to show it to me."

"Pete, it's cool that you like my stories, but I don't want you to know *all* of them."

She crawls to the foot of the futon and picks up a video from the stack on the small Sony TV, *Chasing Amy.*

"Again?" he says.

"*Please.*"

Winter loves the postsex scene where Ben Affleck asks Joey Lauren Adams, "Why me?" and she talks about the search for someone who "gets you" and explains how "thorough" she was in her search. Winter always cries during this.

Would You Like Fries with That Plea Bargain?

"HERE'S MY N.O.A.," Shane Sundfell says, handing Pete a Notice of Appearance on the Keith Johnson case.

Pete and Scott are sitting in "the pit," a crowded open area between courtrooms filled with two dozen mismatched desks and chairs. The space is used by prosecutors and defense attorneys for pretrial conferences, which is a set day for attorneys to discuss and negotiate cases, though most of the time is spent in random chatter. Around them conversations buzz with phrases like, "low end of the range," "drop the firearm enhancement," "he's trying to turn his life around," and "I was only three over par going into the back nine."

"Scott," Pete says, "have you two met?"

"Not officially."

"Shane Sundfell," Sundfell says, extending his hand. Scott stands and shakes it, then sits back down.

"Mr. Sundfell is Satan," Pete says to Scott.

"I know," Scott says.

Sundfell chuckles.

Pete is not kidding. Sundfell and his three associates—known as Beelzebub, the Minion, and Satan's Little Helper—are the most loathed attorneys in the county. They made their name by specializing in child molesters, and the occasional garden variety rapist or murderer, and branched out into a civil practice that includes suing other lawyers.

Sundfell is best known for a three-hour cross-examination of a twelve-year-old rape victim that ended with her crying and walking off the stand and curling up in a ball on the floor of the marble hallway and refusing to testify any further. The defendant was acquitted. Pete was the second-chair prosecutor. Sundfell sits. "So," he says, "are you both on this case? It's going to take two of you to shepherd this dog?" When Pete does not react, Sundfell continues, "You don't really want to go to trial on something this lame, do you?"

"No. I want your client to step forward like a man and take responsibility."

Sundfell chuckles.

"I'm thinking Rape 3," Pete continues, "high end of the range. You can argue for low." The standard sentencing range for Rape 3 is six to twelve months, while the range for Rape 2 is seventy-eight to one-hundred and two months.

"He's innocent."

"Oh, Jesus."

"I'm serious. Think about this, guys. She's drunk—she admits she's drunk. She goes to his place by choice. He's a local rocker. She's a groupie. They have sex. She tells him to put on a condom. What's he do? He stops to put one on! But the mood has passed, they're both drunk, and they go to sleep. Come on, guys, that's not rape. That's *regret*. She regrets having sex with him, feels used, which she probably was, but we're all in trouble if we're going to call it rape every time a woman regrets sex."

Sundfell is making a clumsy stab at male bonding, which Pete always resents in this context. Still, he wants to hear the defense theory of the case, so he encourages Sundfell to continue.

"What about the scratches on his back, and the bruising on her legs?"

"Rough sex. So what?"

"And that explains the bruising near his eye?"

"I'll have to ask Keith about that."

Translation: We'll make something up to explain it.

"And the torn underwear?"

"Can happen when people are ripping clothes off."

"And why did your client say he was out of condoms when his apartment is chock full of them."

"Like he told the detective, he was drunk, he missed them, he couldn't find them."

Pete nods. "And why did your client first say there was no intercourse, then say there was in the taped statement?"

"Okay, that's a problem. I know. But he was *drinking,* he was *smashed.* He doesn't remember things exactly, but he knows he didn't rape her."

"Actually, he said it was possible it wasn't consensual."

"Well, now he's going to say it definitely was consensual."

"So why does she say otherwise?"

"Who knows? Regret, like I said. Also, she was wasted. And I'm going to have witnesses who saw her that night and are going to say it was more than just alcohol."

"Have you got witnesses who saw her do drugs?"

"Not yet."

Translation: My client has friends who will lie if necessary.

"And so she made this all up? Why exactly?"

"Maybe she really believes she was raped, but that doesn't make it rape. You've charged Rape 2, which requires you to prove forcible compulsion. Even Rape 3 requires that she communicate clearly that she doesn't want to have sex."

Pete nods.

Sundfell continues. "Maybe she really didn't want to have sex, but she *never* communicated that to my client, not until she told him to put on a rubber, *and he stopped when she told him that*—and she admits that. You know what?" Sundfell is righteous now. "I should just take this to trial. The more I hear myself, the more I realize, this is a winner at trial. I'd *love* to kick your ass in trial with this case—the facts are on my side, and it's not often the facts are on a defense attorney's side, so I should *leap* at this opportunity to try a winner, but I've been doing this a while and I know that a jury can do fuckin' anything. So to spare my client that risk, even though it's a minimal one, I'll advise him to accept a plea, *if* it's an offer he'd be insane not to take."

"What did you have in mind?"

"Well . . ."

"Just say it."

"Assault 4 with sexual motivation."

A misdemeanor.

"*That's* what you have in mind?" Scott says. "Pete will suck your dick before we give you a misdemeanor."

"Rape 3," Pete repeats. He is thinking he would give an Assault 2 with sexual motivation if that sounds better to Sundfell.

"I won't plead him to a felony, not if it's a sex crime or there's sexual motivation. I want a misdemeanor. You can justify an Assault 4 under these facts. And think of this"—Sundfell tries to smile but cannot muster anything approaching genuineness— "you can avoid pissing off all your comrades you're about to piss off."

Cheap and clumsy. "Let's set it for trial." Pete opens his calendar to pick a date.

"I'm going to want to interview your witnesses," Sundfell says, checking his own calendar.

Translation: I'm going to make some money before I plea bargain in earnest.

"And I'm going to have some motions," he continues.

Translation: I'm going to piss on the truth like it's a fire in my shorts.

"And I'll get a witness list to you as soon as I know who they will be."

Translation: I'm going to hide evidence from you for as long as I can get away with.

They agree on dates for the omnibus hearing, motions, witness interviews, and trial.

"One more thing," Scott says to Sundfell.

"Yes?"

"We all know you're a circus act, but this man"—Scott gestures to Pete—"is an artist. And I don't want to see you trying to drag him down to your level. I, on the other hand, am looking forward to rolling in the muck with you."

Sundfell stares at Scott, then Pete. "You're going to lose this one. I try to never say that, but I'm saying it here." He picks up a scheduling order. "I'll have my client sign for the dates."

"No matter what happens," Scott says to Sundfell's back, "we're still going to win on style points."

Pete says, "Nice negotiating tactics there, Foss."

Al and Sunni, prosecutors at nearby desks, make pained faces as Sundfell exits the room.

"Cooties," Al says.

"You guys have total cooties now," Sunni says. "Go wash up."

"Can't we have the cops plant drugs on him or something?" Scott suggests.

Sundfell does not bring out the best in people.

"That was as gentlemanly as I've ever seen him," Pete says. "He knows some things we don't know—he's going to bushwhack us."

" 'One able to gain victory by modifying his tactics in accordance with his enemy may be said to be divine.' "

"Are you the one who borrowed the Sun Tzu book and never returned it?"

"I figured after a couple months you probably bought another. So who's going to do opening statement?"

"You."

"What are you going to do?"

"Flirt with the judicial assistant or the court reporter."

"What's up? You don't seem psyched to try this case."

"I've got some other things going on."

"Like what?"

Pete lowers his voice. "Well, I'm getting married."

"You're getting *what*ed?"

"Married."

Scott appears alarmed. "When?"

"Don't know."

"To whom?"

"Not sure."

"Okay." Scott considers. "So, want to go out and chase some new tonight?"

Wishin' and Hopin'

SCOTT PICKS up Pete in his black 1985 Dodge Diplomat with all the luxury options, including a Plexiglass bug screen bolted to the front grill.

"I don't feel like going to the Croc," Pete says. "Or the Cha Cha. Or the Lava Lounge. Or Linda's. Or the Five Point or the Baltic Room or the Mecca or the Speakeasy or . . . anywhere we're going to run into the usual suspects."

"Hey, I've got things handled."

Scott parks in the Diamond lot just east of the Pioneer Square totem pole, which leaves them a short walk to the entrance of the Back Door Ultra Lounge on James Street.

They pay a four-dollar cover to a man in a white dinner jacket. As they step up the seedy staircase, they hear the music, a full orchestra backing Frank Sinatra, who's singing *This town is a love-you town, and a shove-you town . . ."*

They ascend to the main floor and make their way to the bar. Several men wear suits, mostly vintage fifties style, and skirts and sweaters seem the preferred look for women.

Scott, who does not wear suits to the office unless he's in trial, wears a light-blue tropical suit with thin lapels and a tie clip. Pete wears his normal navy-blue and has the feeling he is the only person in the room wearing the same clothes now as he was wearing eight hours earlier.

"Johnnie Walker Black, and a Jack and Coke," Scott yells. "Doubles."

On the television above the bar Frank Sinatra is looking dapper in the driver's seat of a late-fifties convertible. Dean Martin is on the passenger's side, one hand around a curvacious blonde, the other clutching a flask. Sinatra is keeping beat on the wheel to a song Pete cannot hear. The scene strikes Pete as the perfect image of the bachelor life: friends, women, drink— *possibilities.*

Scott hands Pete a glass that sports the purple-and-gold UW emblem. "Very fifties," Scott explains.

The drink is strong, so Pete does not complain.

"See," Scott says, knocking a Lucky Strike out with a practiced one-handed move. "This place is what you're looking for." Scott lights up with a Zippo. "The whole retro thing. You might be on the cutting edge with this marriage idea. It's making a comeback. *Everything's* making a comeback—marriage, adultery, promiscuity, alcoholism, Sinatra, the things that made this a great country."

Pete wonders if he should take Scott's keys.

"And there's some talent here tonight," Scott adds.

"I think I'm going to have to adjust my standards," Pete says, "now that I'm looking to get married."

"*What* standards? Two tits and a heartbeat?"

Pete notices a woman alone, cigarette in mouth, checking her purse for matches.

"Zippo," Pete says to Scott.

Scott, who saw the same thing, hands the Zippo off as quick as a surgeon.

Pete flicks the Zippo and carries the flame to her. She finds her matches at about the same time she sees the light. After a moment's hesitation, she palms the matches and leans toward the Zippo and sucks in the flame.

She wears black Capri pants, locally known as clamdiggers, and a white blouse and long faux pearls. Straight hair falls to her chin, frames her high cheekbones. Though she's Caucasian, there's a streak of something else Pete can't quite place. Cameron Diaz's vague ethnicity comes to mind.

"Thanks," she says.

"You're welcome."

They lock eyes and he decides she's flirting with him, though he could not possibly specify why he has this idea.

A moment later a guy who's an inch or two her junior, five-six or so, arrives with two martinis. Pete gives her a going-away smile and crosses back to Scott, returns the Zippo.

"That guy's earring is very un-fifties," Scott says, a bit too loudly.

"Let's not get into a fistfight."

"Leave her for future reference. It's too early in the evening to get committed."

Scott leads into the main lounge area, which calls to mind an oversized suburban rec room complete with bad cheap art, mismatched couches, large stuffed chairs, and an open area of linoleum near the jukebox. Pete nods hello to the singer of the Dudley Manlove Quartet, who is drinking alone, slumped over in a faux La-Z-Boy.

Only one couple is dancing. The man is wearing white pants, topsiders, a blue blazer, and a skipper's cap. He leads a gal in a summer dress to Dusty Springfield's "Wishin' and Hopin'."

"Poor bastard," Scott says, nodding to the blue-blazered man. "Must have lost his yacht."

They take seats at the edge of the dance floor. Several brightly colored ashtrays sit on the coffee table in front of them, along with vintage copies of *Esquire* and *Vogue*.

"Things will pick up later," Scott says.

"You have much success here?"

"Why else would I come back?"

Scott downs his drink, hails a waitress who is wearing a full-length cocktail dress and motorcycle boots.

"Hi," she says. "What can I get you?"

"Where have I seen you before?" Scott asks. "Do you work somewhere else?"

"I used to work at Deja Vu."

Deja Vu is a downtown strip club favored by local musicians and businessmen.

"You look different," Scott says.

"Clothes."

"Do you happen to know Beth Keller?" Pete asks. "I heard she used to work at Deja Vu."

"The name sounds familiar. What was her stage name?"

"Stage name? I don't know."

"I didn't know the real names of most of the girls."

"And what's *your* name?" Scott asks.

"Shannon."

"Shannon, I'm Scott, and this is Pete."

"Nice to meet you both."

"Do you know why Clinton wears boxer shorts?" Scott says.

"To keep his ankles warm."

"We're going to get along swell, Shannon. What's the tattoo? Serpent?"

"Yeah," she says, turning toward Scott so he can get a better look at the black-and-green snake that wraps all the way around her arm just above the elbow, apple in its mouth.

"Cool," Scott says.

"Thanks. So what can I get you?"

"A Johnnie Walker Black and a Jack and Coke. Doubles."

"You got it," she says, smiling at Scott as though he isn't a pig before walking away.

"What the hell?" Pete says to Scott.

"What?"

"How do you get away with that?"

"She really did look familiar. And cocktail waitresses *always* work another job, or they're students or something."

"So are you going to spend the night hitting on her?"

"Intermittently. It's always good to have a back-up plan." Scott stubs out his cigarette. "But you can have her if you want her. I mean, you're the one looking to get married and I don't want to be a home wrecker."

"Thanks, but I don't think she's marriage material."

"How do you know? You haven't slept with her yet."

Pete picks up the *Vogue*. On the cover is a beautiful girl with dark hair that curls just as it touches her sweater-clad shoulders. She has sea-foam green eyes and perfect white skin with just a slight blush on her perfect cheekbones.

"She probably looks like *hell* by now," Scott says, pointing to the cover girl. "And is miserable about it."

"Or maybe she's married with kids and a house and a Range Rover and she's happy."

"Or maybe she's already committed suicide."

Sinatra, a clear deejay favorite, comes on again. "*When I was twenty-one, it was a very good year . . .*"

Perfect drinking and smoking music, Pete thinks as he chases a drag of his cigarette with a long pull of his drink.

When the song finishes, he turns to Scott. "Would you like to be young again?"

"I *am* young."

"Younger."

"Well, yeah, I guess it would be nice to be fifteen again, so I could sleep with fifteen-year-olds."

"How *sweet,*" Shannon says, quickly returning with their two doubles, in Chevron glasses this time.

"Thanks," Pete says, paying for both and tipping well as a sort of an apology for Scott.

"So," Scott says, "where you from, Shannon?"

"Woodinville."

"Woodinville High School?"

"Afraid so."

"And you moved to Capitol Hill after you graduated?"

"Yeah, started taking classes at Seattle Central."

Scott nods. "That's a pretty convincing story," he says, assuming the voice of a skeptical detective.

"Pieces fit together pretty well," Pete agrees in the same tone.

Shannon laughs. "Where are you guys from?" She sets down her drink tray, taps a cigarette out of her pack of Camel Lights.

"Native," Pete says.

"Tacoma," Scott says, lighting her cigarette.

"*Everyone* from Tacoma moves here."

"For good reason," Scott says. "So where do you and your friends hang when you go out?"

"The Re-Bar, the Art Bar, 2218, sometimes the Downunder."

"Where do you think the best place to pick up women is?"

"Elliott Bay Books or any grocery store."

"What do you think our chances are here?"

"You guys should actually do pretty well. About midnight everyone's wearing alcohol goggles."

Scott grins. "That *is* when I look my best."

"You don't look too bad without."

"When did you say you get off work?"

Shannon laughs, puts her cigarette in her mouth, picks up her tray, and moves on.

Scott turns to Pete. "Well, now we gotta get *you* a woman."

"That was a Todd Rundgren song."

Scott ignores this and stares at the ass of a girl who walks by in hip-huggers, then turns back to Pete. "You, my friend, are sitting pretty right now."

"How so?"

"Did you ever see that Woody Allen movie where he talks about marriage being the death of hope?"

"*Annie Hall?*"

"I'm not sure. Maybe it's not a Woody Allen movie. Anyway, the point is that when we're single we have the hope we will someday meet our true love. But as soon as you actually meet your true love, that's it. Your hope is gone." He pours the last ice cube from his glass into his mouth and chews. "And hoping is better than having."

"Thanks for that pep talk at this critical juncture in my romantic life."

Musicians Don't Dance

BY MIDNIGHT Pete and Scott are leaning against the wall next to the jukebox as Dean Martin sings, "*You're nobody until somebody loves you . . .*" Though the new position is a tactical improvement, they do not seem to be using it to great advantage as most of their dialogue is still being wasted on each other.

"I'm not used to working in teams," Scott says. He is just this side of slurring. "I mean," he says, "when we were younger it was the better approach. Girls were always with a friend, and you needed a wingman to peel them off. But as you get older, I think flying solo is a better bet."

Scott then leans against the jukebox, but miscalculates and stumbles, banging his elbow hard on the glass top. "Whoa, didn't spill a drop," he says, righting himself, holding up his glass.

"I saw that," Shannon says, smiling as she walks by.

"My back-up plan is looking better with each passing minute," Scott says to Pete.

Pete, however, is focused on Smoking Girl With Pearls who has entered the area. She is still with the guy who bought her the drink, but another guy has joined them.

"Talent at twelve o'clock high," Scott says.

"I know. Don't leer."

"Why don't you try to take her peacefully," Scott suggests "and if that doesn't work, start swinging. I'll back you."

Pete tries to gauge the relationships between Smoking Girl With Pearls and the two men. Is one her boyfriend? Are the two of them boyfriends?

Dino finishes, and the next song starts with a horn riff Pete recognizes but can't quite place, and then Perry Como's voice booms out, *"The bluest skies you've ever seen in Seattle . . ."*

With exaggerated but genuine enthusiasm the crowd responds to "Seattle," better known as the "Here Come the Brides" TV-show theme song. The dance floor quickly fills and the sur-rounding drinkers turn to watch and many nod along with the beat and some mouth the words.

"Full of dreams to last the years in Seattle . . ."

Pete considers writing an "I Saw U" ad for Smoking Girl With Pearls and then, suddenly, he recalls a girl with perfect ankles sit-ting outside Sean and Jon's Bar on Melrose when he was in Los Angeles. He noticed her, lusted for her, but walked right by and never saw her again. He wonders if the Girl With Perfect Ankles was the love of his life and he blew it.

He drains his glass, sets it down, starts walking.

Smoking Girl With Pearls is watching the frolicking on the dance floor when Pete taps her on the shoulder with the hand holding his cigarette. Ash falls on her white blouse.

She turns, does not notice the ash.

"You want to dance?" he asks as he discreetly drops his ciga-rette butt.

She stares at him for a beat.

One of her escorts also checks him out, but the other pays him no mind.

"I don't really dance," she finally says.

"Neither do I."

She looks at him like he's insane.

He stalls by tapping out a Camel from his crumpled pack, then offers her one.

She holds up the cigarette she is already smoking.

"Never too soon to switch to unfiltereds," is all he can think to say.

She laughs, apparently crediting him with wit rather than drunkenness. He lights a cigarette, narrowly avoids exhaling smoke in her face.

"Last call," the deejay says. "Last, last call for alcohol."

"Are you going to offer me a drink?" she asks.

Trick question?

He looks at her.

She smiles.

"Would you like a drink?" he says, as though the idea is all his.

"Yes, thank you."

She drops her cigarette and grinds it out. Pete admires her ankles.

He takes her hand and leads her toward the bar and her hand squeezes back in some kind of code he isn't sure how to decipher.

"We've got to fight through the dance floor to get to the bar," she points out.

This is an uncannily accurate appraisal of the situation, one that did not occur to Pete.

He drops his cigarette and takes both her hands, as though they are about to dance, and then starts sidestepping through the crowd, hopping and stopping and dodging, advancing a few feet at each opening.

They reach the opposite end of the dance floor just as the chorus is climaxing. "*The bluest skies you've ever seen . . .*"

"Martini and a Johnnie Walker Black," Pete says to the bartender, finally dropping her hand when they arrive because there's no sense in alerting her to the cheap thrill he is deriving from this minor contact of flesh.

She pulls a hard pack of Camel Lights from her pants pocket. Pete lights her cigarette.

"I'm Pete Tyler, by the way."

"Pete Tyler? Why do I recognize that name?"

He lights his own cigarette. "It's familiar-sounding."

She looks him over. "Are you in a band?"

"Was."

"What band?"

"Morph."

She smiles. " 'Fremont Bridge Swan Dive.' "

He nods, intrigued by her grasp of local rock-and-roll trivia.

"You signed with a major label, didn't you?"

"Polygram."

"I'm Esmé, by the way." She holds out a hand and they shake.

"Good to meet you."

"So when was this? It was a while back, wasn't it?"

"Started in eighty-six. I was a fifth-year senior at UW." Pete pronounces UW as *U-Dub*. "We played local clubs for a while— the Central, the Rainbow, the Vogue, the Ditto—then went to L.A., then came back."

"Nineteen eighty-six. I was thirteen."

That's a thought. "So you probably haven't heard of most of the bands from back then," he says.

"Oh, I've heard of a couple. The Moberlys, the Young Fresh Fellows, the Cowboys, the Heats, Moving Parts, the Allies, the Dynette Set, Girl Trouble, Life in General, Bikini Kill, Sky Cries Mary, U-Men, Blood Circus, Visible Targets, Gas Huffer, Gruntruck, the Gits, the Melvins, Love Battery, Cat Butt, the Enemy, Coffin Break, Fitz of Depression, Tad, of course, Green River—"

"Okay, okay. But do you know who was in Green River?"

"Mark Arm and Steve Turner, who went on to Mudhoney, and Stone Gossard and Jeff Ament, who went on to Pearl Jam."

"And what other bands did Gossard play for?"

"March of Crimes, Temple of the Dog."

"And who drove the Melvins' van?"

"Cobain, of course."

"And Duff McKagan's band before Guns N' Roses?"

"That's too easy. There were several. Ten Minute Warning, the Silly Killers, the Vains, the Fartz, the Fastbacks."

"And the Fastbacks are . . . ?"

"Lulu, Kurt, and Kim, and the drummer of the month. It's been Mike Musburger lately, a distant cousin of Brent Musburger."

"And where did Lulu, Kurt, and Kim go to high school?"

"Okay . . . you got me. Where?"

"Nathan Hale."

"So did I still pass your local-music history quiz?"

"One more. And you're betting all your winnings on this. Do you know where the word *grunge* came from?"

"Lester Bangs. Used it to describe Kiss. And then Mark Arm, a.k.a. Mark McLaughlin, used it to describe Mr. Epp and the Calculations, his own band. And then, well, you know the rest."

Impressive. "Where are you from?"

"Olympia. It's only about an hour drive. And I got some good fake I.D. about the time I turned sixteen."

"You'd be a champ on rock-and-roll *Jeopardy.*"

"That's why Sub Pop hired me."

"Sub Pop? What do you do there?"

"Miscellaneous mischief," she says. "So what happened with Polygram? How did your records do?"

"There was just that one. Which tells you how it did."

"Well, at least you have a place in music history as one of the first grunge bands."

"Except we weren't really grunge."

Still, the label stuck and Pete wonders if in the end this is what his life will add up to—*Pete Tyler, lead singer for one of the early Seattle grunge bands, was found dead today*—and hopes to God not. While he's thinking this the drinks arrive and he fumbles with his wallet.

Esmé notices a flash of silver. "What's that?"

"What?"

"Is that a *badge?*" she asks, pointing.

He looks at it next to his driver's license like he's never seen it before: DEPUTY PROSECUTING ATTORNEY.

"I'm a lawyer now," he explains. "Deputy prosecutor."

Esmé smiles at this. "I've never gone out before with a guy with a badge," she says. "I can't even remember going out with a guy with a *job.*"

Pete figures he has blown this. He did not learn enough about her, and he told too much about himself, *and* he did not prepare her for the prosecutor thing.

Rookie mistakes.

Suddenly he realizes she is staring at him.

"I know why I recognized your name," she says. "You're the prosecutor. The one prosecuting Keith Junior?"

He nods.

"Wow," she says flatly.

"I was hoping to avoid that subject tonight."

"You know he was with Sub Pop?"

"Yeah. Publicity should be good for sales."

Pete cannot read the look she's giving him, but it has a questioning edge he is not comfortable with.

She finally says, "That must be weird for you. Prosecuting Keith."

"Yeah, I guess it is if I think about it."

Esmé finishes her drink and picks up the olive on the toothpick and uses her lips rather than her teeth to remove the olive, which she lolls around in her mouth before swallowing. He is dying to kiss those lips.

Suddenly "Retro World" by the Black Halos blasts out and it's a couple notches louder than the lounge music and a few decades newer—a gruff reminder that it's 1999 and one more night is done and gone.

"Time to go home," the deejay adds over the music for those that are too drunk to get it. "You can't fuck or sleep here."

Another night of bright expectations darkened? Pete takes a long drag of his cigarette and wonders if he should bother trying to wrangle a phone number.

"How about a nightcap?" Esmé says.

Suddenly the night is young.

The Rules

AS THEY walk south on Jackson Street the drizzle turns to rain and Pete takes Esmé's hand and they start jogging and her red plaid raincoat flies open like a cape. Pete's raincoat is still in the Dodge Diplomat, probably soon to be silent witness to all sorts of unoriginal sins.

They run across Main Street as darkly clothed bat-cavers emerge from the Catwalk Club, the best place in town for a public flogging until recently when the Health Department ordered an end to the recreation-slash-entertainment.

Pete hails a STITA taxi that cuts in front of a Yellow Cab. As they settle into the back seat, Esmé pulls her feet up one at a time to check the damage to her leather flats. Small rivulets of water run down her forehead and cheekbones. Suddenly the rush of being in the company of an attractive woman runs through Pete and he feels wide awake.

They stop a few blocks past Occidental Park. Pete pays the cabbie and they disembark in front of an old brick building with a wrought-iron gate that leads into a courtyard.

Her apartment is a second-floor studio with polished hardwood floors, wood cabinet hi-fi, another wood cabinet with a TV, a wet bar with old-fashioned martini shakers, and in front of the couch is a kidney-shaped coffee table. The brass bed is near the tall arched windows. Pete is impressed by her sense of decorating style, as he has none.

"Very movie-setish," he says.

"Very cheap," she says. "It's all thrift-store stuff. What can I get you to drink? Scotch?"

"And water, please."

She steps away into what Pete presumes to be the bathroom. He goes straight to her hi-fi cabinet, which houses vinyl, CDs, and books. Pete generally likes to seek clues as to who he is about to sleep with from such evidence.

The CDs are weighted toward promotional freebies from Sub Pop, but also include a few from PopLlama, including the first two Young Fresh Fellows LPs on one disc, favorites of Pete's, and Sleater-Kinney's *The Hot Rock,* from the Olympia label Kill Rock Stars, one of those albums Pete feels he should listen to but never has. Other indie CDs include Liz Phair's *Exile in Guyville,* Elliot Smith's *XO,* Sunny Day Real Estate, Quasi, Juno, and Modest Mouse. The major labels are represented by standard fare such as the Dandy Warhols, Oasis, Garbage, Fiona Apple, and the Cranberries' *To the Faithful Departed,* which—because of the songs "Hollywood" and "I'm Still Remembering"—happens to be the only Cranberries album Pete likes. He picks up and examines a heavy brass Space Needle replica separating the CDs from the books.

"When I was a little kid I wanted to live in Seattle," Esmé says, returning from the bathroom, crossing to the bar. "Because I thought if I lived in Seattle I would be living in the Space Needle."

Pete sets back the replica and skims the book spines: Clark Humphrey's *Loser,* Ann Beattie's *Distortions,* Raymond Carver's *What We Talk About When We Talk About Love,* A. M. Homes's *The Safety of Objects,* and, oddly, Bret Easton Ellis's *American Psycho.* She also has hardcovers, including *Bridget Jones's Diary, A Certain Age,* and *The Rules,* subtitled: *Time-Tested Secrets for Capturing the Heart of Mr. Right.* He holds this small pinkish best-seller up toward Esmé.

"Gift," she explains, as she puts ice into a shaker. "Ironic gift. A 'rules girl' would never bring a boy she just met home."

"A rules girl?"

"A rules girl, according to the authors, is someone who follows 'The Rules.' Things like 'Don't accept a Saturday night date after Wednesday, and don't call a man, and don't even return his phone call, and don't open up too fast.' " She pours vodka and vermouth into the shaker. "I'm more of a break-the-rules girl."

She shakes the martini. He watches her breasts.

After setting the book back, he steps over to the window. Between buildings he can see a slice of Elliott Bay and a glimmer of moonlight as the cloud layers float across the sky. He guesses by the brightness of the light that the moon must be full. Esmé hands him a scotch as she passes on her way to the hi-fi.

The distinct scratch of a needle on vinyl hisses out and Pete instantly recognizes the opening horns of Petula Clark's "Sign of the Times."

"You can buy this on CD now," Esmé says, "but I haven't got around to it."

She joins Pete at the window and cracks it open. He lights her cigarette.

"It's a sign of the times, and I know that I won't have to wait much longer . . ."

Pete loves cheese-fest pop songs and finds it interesting that Esmé chose this one.

"How did you end up a lawyer?" she asks. "Didn't know what else to do with your life?"

"Exactly."

"Seriously, why did you become a lawyer?"

"Long story."

"Short version."

"I was about to turn thirty."

Pause.

"How about the medium-length version?" She blows a thin stream of smoke outside the window. "Like what happened with the band?"

"We came back up here from L.A. when things were starting to happen, and I saw all the other bands play. Some really sucked. But a couple blew me away, and I realized: they meant it, and we didn't. We just started a band to get girls, which I think is true for most bands, but we never got beyond that. "They say everyone's got one novel in them? Well, we had one album in us, and that was it. So the band broke up, Bob died, I went to law school. The lawyer thing was just a stall at first, but then I found out I happened to be good with juries, which intrigued me. And now I'm hooked." He lights a Camel.

"I probably should be careful about mentioning you to anyone at work," she says. "There would be too many questions. About the case."

"Do people talk about it a lot at Sub Pop?"

"Poneman asked us not to. So of course we do."

"What's the general sentiment?"

"That it's a gray area."

"What do you think?"

"I don't know. I've only heard a lot of people talking."

She turns and steps over to the couch, puts her cigarette out in an oversized glass ashtray stolen from Tini Bigs. Pete waits a beat, then follows. He puts his arm on the back of the couch, not quite touching her shoulder. She pulls her legs up underneath her and rests her head back against his arm. He is aching to skip the chitchat and just grab her skinny body and carry her to bed and . . .

"I have to tell you," she says. "I'm not sure yet what I think of this."

"What?"

"That you're a *prosecutor*. And you're prosecuting Keith." When he does not respond, she continues. "Does your family think it's strange? That you're a prosecutor now? They probably think it's great."

"Well, my mother has never really said anything about it, and my father's dead."

"Oh, I'm sorry."

"It's been ten years. Car crash. Drunk driving."

"A drunk driver?"

"Him."

"Oh." She looks at him. "Sorry."

Pete stubs his cigarette out. "So what about you?" he asks. "What do your parents think about your occupation?"

"They'd like me to meet someone who's a grown-up. Which I never do in the music business." She pauses. "You know, I appreciate you showing interest and all, but I'm already interested."

Pete is not sure about the grammatical leap from him showing interest in her to her being interested in him, but he gets the idea.

"But when I hold your hand I know you couldn't be the way you used to be . . ."

"Great horn arrangement," he says, which is not among the most seductive things he's ever said.

He leans in slowly and kisses her lightly, his eyes open. Her eyes close. He kisses her again, still softly, lingering. She puts her hand around his neck. One of his hands slides to the back of her neck while the other slides over her Capri pants and under the untucked blouse to the small of her back. Her kisses become more insistent. He changes the rhythm by breaking it off and initiating a series of quicker kisses.

"I'd like you to spend the night," she says during one of the breaks, her lips staying within an inch of his. "If you don't mind just snuggling and going to sleep."

Like that's going to happen. "Sounds good."

The Moon
at Three A.M.

PETE LISTENS to the rain's rhythm on the fire escape. The bathroom door opens and there's a flash of light and then the light clicks off and he hears Esmé padding over to the bed.

She is wearing nothing but white panties. This does not strike Pete as wise if she truly plans not to have sex. Her breasts are smallish and well shaped and pointing over his head and the sight arouses him.

He puts his arm out as she eases into bed and rests her head on his chest. He smells vanilla body lotion, inhales deeply, appreciates the scent. Her leg slides over his own, then her knee moves toward his groin. Here she cannot ignore what he has in mind.

She lifts her head off his chest, kisses him quickly.

"Good night," she says.

"Good night."

She moves her leg off his, but places her head back on his chest, drapes her arm over. "Do you mind if I cuddle against you," she says.

"No, of course not." *I enjoy torture.*

He considers his options. The adrenaline rush of initial contact has ebbed and the alcohol is wearing off and what better time to be a gentleman? Usually he has trouble sleeping with a woman up against him, but right now he welcomes the warmth.

He turns over onto his right side, taking her left hand. She spoons up against him. Her smooth thigh gently presses against the back of his own. He feels her breath on his neck and he wants her, but maybe if he rests for a few seconds first . . .

Suddenly Pete is shaken awake. He takes this to mean he fell asleep at some point.

"Pete?"

There is a beautiful girl beside him and this is wonderful news.

"Hey."

"Hey."

He remembers her and much of the night, which is not always the case, and does not recall anything especially embarrassing, which is definitely not always the case.

"Look," she says, gesturing to the window. "The moon."

The rain has stopped and scattered clouds blow in from the south, thin cirrus clouds floating past the higher, darker nimbus clouds, and the whole tableau is dramatically shaded by the weirdly bright full moon.

"Cool," is the first word that comes to mind.

She hands him a bottle of water, which he gratefully drinks from. They lean against the bars of the brass bed, stare at the moon. He is surprised that he does not feel too bad.

"I'm curious," she says. "Why aren't you married yet?"

Pete has a sudden image of himself standing in the middle of a road, headlights bearing down on him out of darkness, antlers on his head.

"All I mean," she says, "is that I'm surprised you're not. You seem like somebody who would be snapped up."

"When I was in a band, I didn't want to get married."

"And now?"

"And now I'm not in a band." He hands her back the water.

"Do you have any kids?"

"Not as far as I know," he says with what he hopes plays as humor. Off her look he adds, "No, no kids."

"Girlfriend?"

"Not really."

"In other words, you do."

He reaches for his pack of Camels and lights a cigarette, figuring it might mask his questionable breath. "There's this gal I see, but it's not too serious."

"FTF."

"FTF?"

"Friends that fuck."

He smiles. "Something like that."

"A guy like you should have a girlfriend." She takes a long drink of water, moistens her lips. "Is there something wrong with you?"

"Not as far as you know."

She laughs. "When was your last serious girlfriend?"

"What?"

"Your last serious girlfriend?"

"Serious? Probably the one in L.A."

"What happened?"

"The band had to leave L.A." He puts out the cigarette after a long drag.

"And you haven't had a girlfriend since you moved back here several years ago?"

"Girlfriends, yes," he says. "But nothing serious."

"Why not?"

"Haven't met anyone who noticed the moon at three A.M."

She smiles and sets down the bottle of water. "Good answer. But I was going to fuck you anyway."

She lightly bites his neck, then starts kissing down his chest as her hand lightly scratches across his stomach. He kisses the top of her head and though her hair smells like smoke it also smells like shampoo and perfume, and the mix works. She moves her fingertips around his stomach in a slow circle and he closes his eyes and enjoys the curative sensation of human contact.

Her hand sweeps slightly lower down his stomach with each circle and his relaxation kicks over into arousal. He wraps an arm around her back, lightly caresses the curve of her breast, kisses the nape of her neck. She bites his nipple and then blows warmly on it and his stomach tightens hard. He runs a hand through her hair.

Her face then turns up to him and her lips move to his, and at the same moment her hand moves under his boxer shorts. His hands take her by the chest, just below her breasts, and he rolls her over and she pushes up against him as he moves on top.

Breakfast at Esmé's

STILL LYING in bed, Pete picks up the torn condom foil wrapper from the floor: Natural X lambskin. Not particularly effective against STDs; more so against pregnancy, which is Pete's main worry. He puts the wrapper in the ashtray, thinking himself an exemplary overnight guest for this.

Outside it is raining and the morning is soft gray. Pete hated waking up in L.A. to the harsh angling sun. When he lived in Venice for a few months he bought blackout curtains and painted his bedroom walls black. This improved his sleep, if not his general mood.

Esmé is in the kitchen, back to him, wearing the white and blue striped pajamas she forgot to don last night. Bacon and toast and coffee and other comforting smells waft over to him.

"Do you want some orange juice?" she asks.

"Do I have time for a quick shower?"

"Sure. This omelette thing may go horribly wrong."

He turns the water as hot as he can bear for a few minutes and then turns it to a cold blast for about half a minute, his standard morning recovery routine. After, he brushes his teeth with an Interplak device.

Esmé looks beautiful without makeup and she is not awkward about last night's hijinx. Pete is grateful for both of these things. The food is good and they talk about normal small things, like movies and books and an article in the *Seattle Weekly* trashing Microsoft.

When she is in the bathroom he writes down her phone number from the phone hanging on the kitchen wall. As a matter of habit, he prefers this to asking for a phone number as it preserves the element of surprise if he decides to call.

They kiss goodbye at her door. If she finds it odd he has not asked for her number it does not show.

"Thanks for breakfast."

"Anytime."

"Tomorrow?"

She laughs.

Outside, the rain has stopped and the clouds are breaking up. The sun shines from above Beacon Hill, glittering off the wet streets, and Pete wishes he had his Ray-Bans, but it is easy to forget your sunglasses when you live in Seattle.

At the corner of Second and Cherry he stops for a breath and gazes west at Elliott Bay and the white morning moon hanging over the Olympic Mountains. A vague sense of calm contentment comes over him and once again his faith in the redemptive power of passion is affirmed.

He looks up at the sound of a commercial airliner as it banks into a swooping turn on the landing approach over Elliott Bay toward Sea-Tac Airport, and this calls to mind the The, "*You watch a plane flying across the clear blue sky, this is the day your life will surely change . . .*"

He wonders if he has just met his future bride, and the possibility spooks him, but he shakes it off and just enjoys the morning-after buzz. He figures even if he never sees her again he at least has this buzz and it is worth having.

Visible Injuries

AMBER IS examining a large stuffed purple dinosaur with Carrie Findley-Orness, a victims' advocate, when Pete enters the conference room with Scott. Amber sets down the dinosaur. Pete holds out his hand. "Pete Tyler."

Amber stands and shakes his hand. She is tallish, quite thin, and almost beautiful despite the dark bags under her eyes. Her torn Levi's are baggy and her T-shirt is tight and she's not wearing a bra, which suggests to Pete that they might have to discuss courtroom attire.

Scott introduces himself after Pete.

"Better known as the insensitive twins," Carrie jokes to Amber, scoring a smile.

They all sit at the conference table surrounded by stuffed animals and toys, and also video equipment, which the children prefer playing with.

"As Carrie probably told you," Pete says, trying not to sound too official, "we're the deputy prosecutors handling this case."

"She said you guys are the best."

"I'd have to agree with that," Scott contributes.

Pete explains the posture of the case, distinguishes reality from TV law, and wraps up by saying he thinks there is still a chance for a plea.

"So you're going to offer a plea bargain?"

"We already have."

"You *have*?" Amber looks at Carrie, Scott, then back at Pete.

"It was turned down," Pete says. "Carrie would have contacted you if it was accepted. We try to keep victims informed about what's going on, but the reality is that we make tactical decisions like that on our own."

Carrie smiles at Amber. "See, I told you these guys are great public servants." This makes Amber laugh, and Pete grateful for Carrie's presence.

"We *do* want to hear what you have to say," Pete tells Amber.

"You want to know what I want?"

"Yes."

"I want an *apology*."

Pete was surprised the first few times he heard this in rape cases but is not anymore. "We could probably work that into the deal. If there is one."

"I can't believe he's *denying* this. I mean, at first I really wasn't sure if I should tell the police, but then I heard he was *lying* about it, and lying about me, and just being . . . a jackass."

Pete nods.

"He knows what he did," she continues. "Does he not think it's wrong, or what?"

"At first he told the detective that you two never had intercourse—"

"*Liar.*"

"And then later he told the detective that you two *did* have intercourse, but he stopped when you asked him to get a condom, and he couldn't find one."

"The weird thing is, he did. He stopped to put on a condom, that's when I ran out. But it's not like he couldn't find one—they're all over the place."

"Why don't you just tell us what happened," Pete says, "starting at the beginning when you saw him at the Breakroom."

Amber does, and the story matches reasonably well with what she told Detective Tuiaia, and this is a good sign. When she gets to the rape she starts to cry, though only a little, and she skims through the details and Pete does not press her because this is not the time for that.

When she's finished, Pete says, "The jury is going to like you and they're going to believe you."

Amber looks up. "You really think so?"

"I do." He often says this, but here he thinks it is true.

Scott and Carrie both nod in agreement.

"We've got a good case," Scott says.

"It's not a problem that I waited a while before talking to police?"

"That's not unusual," Scott says. "And the good thing is that when you finally went to the doctor the injuries to your legs were still visible. The bruising is pretty clear in the Polaroids."

Pete reaches his hand out toward Amber, but does not actually touch her. "I have to ask you something."

"Okay."

"Please don't talk to anyone about what happened between now and the trial. I know it's the kind of thing you want to talk about with friends, but don't. Especially don't talk about it with anyone in the music scene."

"Why not?"

"It's best if you don't talk to *anybody* about this. It could hurt our case."

"Somebody has been calling from *The Stranger*."

"Oh, Jesus, and don't talk to anyone from the media. Trust me on this. Talk to nobody. It's your decision," he remembers to add. "But don't do it."

She looks at him. He looks back. He does not want her to talk about it for two reasons: one, even someone she perceives as a friend could become an adverse witness if she tells them something that is in any way different from what she told police, and the more a story is told, no matter how true, the more the details are likely to change; and, two, she will lose the emotion if she keeps talking about it and he wants her to cry in front of the jury, he wants her to sob, he wants her to be wracked with the pain of a memory she's kept down for weeks.

"Okay," she says. "Maybe it will be better that way."

After Carrie walks Amber out, Scott turns to Pete. "So which one of us is going to date her after this?"

"She's not even twenty-one. She probably doesn't even know who the Brat Pack were."

"Who?"

Pearl Jam vs. Nirvana

"I SHOULDN'T have slept with you that night," Esmé says as Pete opens the Volvo door for her. "What a slut."

He closes the door, smiles at her through the windshield as he walks around to the driver's side. He feels edgy, which he has not felt on a date in years, and he wonders if it is because of an attraction he should heed the meaning of, or simply because of the pressure he has created by viewing his dates as potential mates for life.

Esmé wears a blue skirt, white men's shirt, and the long pearls. Her eyeshadow and mascara are subtle, her lipstick dark red. Pete is relieved to find her as attractive as he remembers.

"I haven't slept with a guy on a first night like that since college," she says as he climbs into the car.

He wonders if she plans to withhold tonight.

"I'm glad you called. Though I'm not supposed to say things like that."

"The 'rules'?"

"Yes, and I shouldn't have agreed to the first night you suggested, either," she says. "But I don't really have time for all that."

"The whole point of that book is to *trick* some guy into wanting you?" he says as he turns onto First Avenue.

"Essentially, yes."

"I've gotta say, I don't really see the point of tricking someone. Aren't they going to figure it out at some point?"

"I believe the logic is that men are too emotionally retarded to understand what they're feeling."

"Oh." *Can't really argue with that.*

Pete usually chooses the car music carefully on dates as music is, of course, key to mood—including his own. He usually opts for something semi-alternative but not too grating. *Nirvana Unplugged* gets the nod tonight.

"So what's the plan?" Esmé asks.

Though Pete is a serial dater, he is not a creative dater. He tends toward a movie and then dinner and drinks, and then sex, or perhaps a live show at the Crocodile and then dinner and drinks, and then sex.

"Dinner," he says. "Drinks."

"I once went on this date where the guy bought a couple pints of Canadian Club and we rode the ferry back and forth from Bainbridge to Elliott Bay drinking."

"You're kidding?"

"Nope."

"*I* used to do that on dates in college."

"*You're* kidding?"

"No. It's been a while, though."

"Well, this was last year. And the guy was about thirty."

"In a band?"

"Of course."

They pass the Lusty with its everchanging marquee, which reads tonight:

ALWAYS OPEN, NEVER CLOTHED

"I've seen that one before," Esmé says.

"When they don't have anything timely, they put that one up."

"Sometimes they're really clever."

"The dancers contribute some of them." Pete decides not to

mention Winter, who has penned a few gems. "What's the first thing a dancer says in the morning?"

"What?"

"It's a joke. What's the first thing a stripper says in the morning?"

"I don't know. What?"

"What band did you say you were in?"

Esmé gives him a small laugh.

During the applause between "About a Girl" and "Come as You Are" Esmé asks, "Who do you like better—Nirvana or Pearl Jam?"

There it is.

Pete was almost expecting the question. A native must choose, of course, and the answer has the same significance as the classic sixties query, "Beatles or Stones?"

"Take your time, hurry up, the choice is yours . . ."

"Okay," he says. "Nirvana."

"Pearl Jam."

Pause.

"Eddie Vedder is sexier than Kurt Cobain," Esmé explains. "Especially since he's alive."

Pete wonders if this disagreement may portend additional, deeper, rifts. However, he decides he respects her preference for the living to the dead.

From Both Sides Now

EL GAUCHO is one of the few Seattle restaurants with valet
parking, which Pete takes a wide U-turn to use. The valet is
about twenty years old and has a goatee and is in a local band,
unsurprisingly enough.

Sara, the hostess, a stylish and pretty student at Seattle Art In-
stitute, greets Pete by name and takes Esmé's coat. She leads
them through the dark open space, which is done in blues and
blacks that contrast with the crisp white tablecloths. They are
seated in Pete's favorite booth, the first in the upper tier against
the north wall.

"What would you like to drink?" Sara asks Esmé.

"Vodka martini, please."

Sara nods and turns to Pete. "I'll have your waiter bring you
a Johnnie Walker Black, unless you would prefer a single malt?"

"Laphroaig, please." *Like God spitting in your mouth.*

Esmé looks around. In the bar the piano man plays a Gersh-
win tune Pete associates with the Zombies as flames cast an orange glow from the open kitchen.

"It's not often I go out to restaurants where no one's going to
be shooting up in the bathroom," Esmé says.

"Don't be so sure they won't be." Pete flashes on Rose, Vomit
Girl from Amazon.com. "How long have you been out of college again?"

"Four years."

"You'll have to excuse me if I ask some of the same questions I already asked that night," he says. "I was drinking a little."

"I totally understand." She pauses. "What was your name again?"

Sara escorts another couple by, smiles at Pete as she passes.

"You bring a lot of dates here?" Esmé asks him.

Yes. "Not really."

"Have you gone out with the hostess?"

"No, she has a boyfriend."

"So you checked it out."

He is surprised how easily he stumbled into that cross-examination setup.

Usually, at this point on a date, Pete has a plan: learn as much as possible about her, reveal as little as possible about himself, and decide what he is willing to do or say to sleep with her.

Here, however, he has already slept with her and, contrary to his experience, this has increased rather than lessened his desire.

And what about the marriage idea?

"What?" she says.

"What?"

"That expression you just had," she says. "What were you thinking? You looked *worried.*"

"Oh, no, just thinking about work." Pete realizes too late that this is the wrong white lie.

"I sparked a few conversations about Keith Junior at the office this week. Wasn't hard to do. Everyone's got an opinion."

Pete leans in. "So what are his friends saying?"

"Well, it's interesting." She also leans in, keeps her voice low. "Some are talking about what a psycho bitch she is, of course. But I talked to Meg, who knows him pretty well, and she thinks he knows he fucked up. She says he just wants to get this over with."

"Plea?"

"I don't know. She says Keith probably doesn't think it should be called rape, even though that's what it was, if that makes sense?"

"It does."

"I'm not trying to spy for you or anything, but I just thought you might want to know that."

Pete nods, considers.

The drinks arrive and Pete and Esmé both sit back. The waiter gives a quick pitch for the specials. Esmé starts with a salad and has the crabcakes appetizer for an entree. Pete is in a New York steak mood, figuring an occasional dose of secondhand steroids can't hurt.

Esmé sips at her martini, leaving a lipstick stain on the glass, an image he remembers from their first night.

"I feel kind of torn here," she says. "On one hand, I'm a traitor to women if I don't take Amber's side, on the other hand I'm a traitor to Sub Pop and the whole arts world if I'm on the side of the prosecutor. You know?"

"I know."

"But I think people should take responsibility for their lives, for what they do. Even musicians. So I can respect your situation—you have to play the grown-up. Unfortunately, a lot of people we both know don't like grown-ups." She smiles. "I do, though."

"Did you know that I'm almost forty?"

Night in White Satin

"IT'S SNOWING," Sara says, holding forth Esmé's coat.

Pete has seen the slushy raindrops that pass for snow and this is what he is expecting when he steps outside with Esmé. Instead, there is a thin sheen of white over the world and good-sized snowflakes blowing about.

"This is *crazy*," Esmé says.

Pete hands his ticket to the valet.

"This is *so* cool." Esmé raises her face to the falling flakes.

There is not much traffic and the few cars on the road drive slowly, the beams of their headlights shining into the whiteness.

Esmé begins spinning, arms out and head back. Pete is totally taken with her in this moment.

The Volvo pulls up, fog lamps ablaze. Esmé stops spinning when the valet opens the passenger door for her.

"Isn't this great?" she says to the valet.

"Driving's a little tricky."

Pete briefly examines his Volvo for damage before handing over a tip.

Everclear's "I Will Buy You a New Life" blasts from 107.7—the valet was apparently rocking out.

"I can't believe Everclear did that moronic Gap ad," Esmé says. "It's not like they needed the money."

"Maybe it's a hedge against getting old."

"Still, it's embarrassing."

"I could click over to the CD. It's always risky listening to the radio. Can't control what the next song might be."

"That's a telling comment."

He picks up the speed as they drive up First Avenue, the flakes sticking to the windshield before they are wiped away. Everclear segues into Blink 182's "Dammit," with the "*so this is growing up*" riff, which Pete takes as an omen.

"Snow in spring," Esmé says. "Do you think this has something to do with the end of the millennium approaching? Has this ever happened before?"

Pete turns down the stereo, pulls his cell phone out of its cradle, and punches in his mother's number.

"Hello?"

"Hi, Mother. It's snowing downtown."

"Here, too. It's pretty, but it's going to kill the rhododendrons."

"When was the last time it snowed in spring?"

"We were in college . . ." The *we* is she and his father. "I think it was 1959. We thought it had something to do with the atomic bomb."

"Nineteen fifty-nine," Pete says to Esmé.

"Who's with you?" his mother asks.

"A date."

"Who?"

"Gotta go, Mother. Just wanted to say hello."

"Drive carefully."

Pete sets the cell phone back.

"That was nice of you to call your mom."

"She likes doling out Seattle trivia. She can tell you the name of every hotel before they were bought out by the chains. The Olympic, now the Four Seasons. The Plaza, now the Westin. All of them. She's very nostalgic about Seattle."

"So that's where it comes from."

"What?"

"The nostalgia?"

"Hey, seems like everyone's nostalgic these days—everyone wants to go back to *something*."

Pete turns the stereo up as they pass the old Vogue, a.k.a. the Vague. He doesn't recognize the band following Blink 182 and so he clicks on the CD player, disc 5, R.E.M.'s *Eponymous*.

"Didn't want to risk the radio anymore?"

"Nope. Never know when they might play that Prince song."

He takes a sliding turn onto Virginia and then a right onto Fifth Avenue under the monorail tracks. The trees up Fifth are ablaze with spidery lights and the road is empty and white with no tire tracks, begging him forward.

Esmé taps her feet as Michael Stipe sings—*"gardening at night . . ."* and whatever else he's mumbling about. Pete likes that she can listen to music and just take the moment.

They drive down the middle of the road, passing Niketown and Eddie Bauer and the Vintage Park, and then an idea comes to Pete. He takes a left on Seneca, another left on Sixth, and drives back toward the Camlin Hotel.

The old elevator smells of wood polish. In the Cloud Room on the top floor there is a new piano player playing a tune Pete cannot quite place. He stops to listen. *". . . and he likes to sing along, and he likes to shoot his gun, but he don't know what it means . . ."*

Pete is horrified by this musical abuse of Nirvana, but Esmé laughs and then he does, too. They move to the bar and he orders a scotch for himself and a martini for her.

They take their drinks outside to the patio and step through the slush up to the north wall, from which they look out on the Space Needle, Queen Anne Hill, Lake Union, and the I-5 bridge completely empty of traffic. The flakes drift slowly, sparkling in lights from the roof a few feet above them. The city is eerily quiet.

"Where would you rather have a house?" Esmé asks. "Queen Anne, with a view of Elliott Bay? Or the southeast side of Queen Anne, with a view of downtown and Lake Union? Or maybe Ballard, with a view of Puget Sound? Or Fremont, with a view of the canal? Or how about Laurelhurst or Leschi, with a view of Lake Washington?"

"Downtown loft," he says.

"I mean five years from now. You're married. And you have children."

"What?"

"Don't panic, it's a hypothetical. You're married and have children."

"Boys or girls?"

"Two girls and a boy."

"Okay."

"Where would your home be?"

"I don't know. I don't know where that would be."

Their breath comes out in clouds that hang and mingle together before dissolving into the white air.

Fears of a Couch

ESMÉ MOVES on top of Pete, keeping one hand on his chest while the other puts him inside of her. She inhales sharply, closes her eyes, and moves her hips to "Sweet Child O' Mine." Though Guns N' Roses' *Appetite for Destruction* is not a customary choice of Pete's for mood-setting romantic music, it is field-testing well. They made out during "Mr. Brownstone," were into heavy foreplay by the time "Paradise City" started, and he was inside her just in time for the opening riff of "Sweet Child O' Mine."

Esmé's head turns from side to side, pearls swinging across her breasts—*"where do we go, where do we go, oh where do we go now"*—and Pete admires her image, which is backlit by the snow fluttering against the window. Pete thinks of Neal Cassady's motto, "Sex is the one and only holy and important thing in life," and it seems true at this moment, particularly with Pete's understanding that sex is music is sex is music.

"God."

"God, yes."

"God *damn* it."

"Fucking *God*."

Pete hopes he doesn't burn in hell.

After, they lie together on the side of the futon near the window and Esmé rests her head on his chest and they watch the swirling snow increase the whiteness outside as the last cut on the album, "Rocket Queen," plays out.

"Listen to what a sentimental kid Axl can be," Esmé says. "I think the song was written for some L.A. chick named Barbi Van-something." She quiets for the finish.

"*. . . Don't ever leave me, say you'll always be there. All I ever wanted was for you to know that I care.*"

"He probably dumped her by the time the album came out," Esmé says.

"Song still works. Sounds like he meant it when he sang it."

Esmé sits up, takes a drink from a bottle of water, then says, "Do you like being a lawyer?"

"I do. I like the storytelling. And I like doing something I'm good at that feels like it matters." He takes the offered bottle and drinks. "But I wasn't ready for it in my twenties. I wasn't ready for *anything* in my twenties."

"I'd like to see you in front of a jury."

"I don't look that cool without a guitar."

Esmé lights a cigarette. Smoke drifts slowly out of her mouth. "I have a confession to make."

Herpes?

Pete sets down the water and reaches for his Camels. Esmé hands him the matches. He lights up.

"I'm supposed to go to law school in the fall."

Worse than herpes.

"Isn't that what you're supposed to do," she continues, "when you don't know what to do with your life?"

"Are you serious? Are you really going to law school?"

"Well, I'm supposed to."

"What do you mean you're supposed to?"

"I'm enrolled."

"Where?"

"I've been accepted to Yale. And also UW. But I figure if I'm going to do it, I might as well do it all the way and go to Yale. I hear UW law school kind of sucks."

"You're serious?"

Esmé nods. "That's why I rushed into this thing with you like some kind of desperate tart."

"Law school." He shakes his head.

"Thing is, I *really* don't want to be a lawyer. At least I don't think I do." She has a drag of her cigarette. "I know it's not like *Ally McBeal* or anything, but I don't really know what it *is* like." Pete takes a beat to picture Calista Flockhart naked.

"It depends," he finally says. "What kind of law are you interested in?"

"I don't know."

"Any idea?"

"No, I don't even know if I want to be a lawyer."

"Well, there are other things you can do with a law degree. Bartending, for example."

Esmé laughs. "I envy our parents," she suddenly says. "They knew how it was supposed to be."

"Didn't always work out that way, though."

"True."

The covers have slipped down to just below Esmé's belly and Pete admires her body. He puts his cigarette in the ashtray and leans down and gives her a quick kiss on a rib just below her breast.

"I'm thinking of moving back in with my parents to save money before I go to school," she says, sliding her fingers through his hair. "I love Seattle and I hate the idea of leaving here. I wish I had a good reason to stay."

He kisses her, tries to end the conversation.

She breaks off the kiss. "I couldn't help but notice the minimal furniture in here."

Pete is not sure where she is going with this, but senses a setup.

"Can't even commit to a couch," she says, "can you?"

He smiles, because what can he say?

This Song Is About You

"BLOW JOB," Scott says, "but no intercourse."

"Would you find that goddam case?"

"I'm looking."

Pete and Scott are in the office library on the tenth floor and Pete is at the computer station looking up cases in Westlaw. They are surrounded by hundreds of law books but these are mostly for atmosphere as it is more efficient to research on the computer. However, when the printer is down, as it is today, the dusty old books come in handy. Pete finds the case citation with the computer and Scott then snags the text.

"We got into an argument that lasted more than an hour," Scott continues as he scans the shelves.

"About her not sleeping with you?"

"No, about that Carly Simon song, 'You're So Vain.' You know, the one that goes, 'You're so vain, you probably think this song is about you.' Well, how can it be vanity if the song really *was* about him? Which it was! The whole goddam argument was right out of a *Seinfeld* episode."

"No wonder she won't fuck you."

"Found it," Scott says, removing a book from the bottom shelf.

Pete punches another query term into the computer. They received a brief from Sundfell seeking to suppress the taped statement because Detective Tuiaia failed to read Miranda rights on the tape itself. The detective read the defendant his Miranda rights, both at the house and at the station just before recording the statement, but Sundfell's brief argues that the Miranda rights must not only be read but that they *must be included on the recording.*

"We're so screwed," Scott announces.

"How?"

"The son of a bitch is right. Miranda rights must be on the tape."

"Or?"

"Or we're screwed."

"Is that what the case says? 'Or the prosecutor is screwed'?"

"Yeah, it's in the headnotes. However, it's a statutory violation rather than a constitutional violation, so we could use the taped statement for impeachment under 613 and *Belgarde.*"

"Let me see."

Scott hands Pete the casebook. "Anyway, she won't fuck me because, quote, 'We never do anything,' unquote. Which is what we somehow ended up discussing, *after* arguing about Carly Simon for a goddam hour. You know that routine? Where she won't tell you what she really wants to argue about, and it just suddenly blurts out and you suddenly realize, *Oh, that's what this is about.*"

"Do you?" Pete says as he skims the case. "Do anything with her?"

"Mostly I've just gone to her house and we've hung around and watched videos and got drunk and I pawed and begged until she placated me."

"So what's she griping about?"

"I don't know." Scott sits on the conference table. "She's a waitress and an artist. She used to be a stripper. It's not like she's some debutante."

"You still might want to try to show her some affection and respect," Pete says without looking up.

"Suddenly *you're* the goddam expert?"

"I've already fucked up more relationships than you'll ever be in."

"Okay, so you've got that going for you."

Pete hands Scott back the casebook. "You're right. We're screwed."

"Thanks to the academic cretins on our Supreme Court. I'd like to see them try a case in the real world."

"Should we try to bait him into testifying just so we can impeach him?"

"They tried that in the O.J. trial, remember? Held back his lying-ass denials to officers so that he would be forced to take the stand to deny it. And now Marcia Clark is known as the most pathetic prosecutor in North America."

"Sundfell is going to be stuck with the no-intercourse theory that his guy told Tuiaia."

"He'll go with whatever lie will fly."

"It's a shame we don't have any semen."

"What kind of son of a bitch stops in the middle of a rape to put on a condom? No wonder he never became a major rock star. No follow-through."

Dawn Lund, the SAU supervisor who has an office next to the library, pokes her face out in the hall, looks at Scott, then Pete, then shakes her head and closes her door.

"Gotta love her for putting up with us," Pete says.

"Devil's advocate for a moment," Scott says. "What if he didn't rape her?"

Pause.

"Then why the lies?" Pete says. "Why the dodgy answers to Tuiaia? And he basically did the same thing to Danielle and God knows how many others."

"It's possible he was so trashed that night that he really doesn't know if he did or not. Remember nights like that? So he decided to admit to it just in case we had evidence. He didn't know we're not going to be able to prove intercourse without ejaculate for a DNA sample."

Pete considers. "Should we offer him a stipulated polygraph? Not with a private polygrapher, but with our guy Barnes."

"Won't do any good if he really doesn't know."

"I bet he knows."

"It'll be inconclusive if he's fuzzy on it."

"So we stipulate that it only comes in if the results are conclusive one way or the other."

Scott nods. "Sounds like a plan."

Pete logs out on the computer, an archaic 486 that takes a few moments.

"How's the marriage thing coming?" Scott asks.

"Working on it."

"What happened with the girl with pearls?"

"Not sure yet."

"You fuck her?"

"Did you *buy* that ugly couch you have, or did somebody *give* it to you?"

"It came with the apartment. Why?"

"Let's get lunch at Once Teriyaki."

Drink & Dial

A WARM front sweeps through and leaves the streets wet and warm and without any sign of snow. Pete, who should be doing trial prep work, goes home early and climbs into the hammock with *The Sportswriter*.

Pete learns he shares something with Mr. Ford—he assumes the author is like the protagonist in this way—a habit of reading catalogues for the odd soothing they provide.

When the truths of the novel start to accumulate an uncomfortable weight, Pete puts down the book and picks up a J. Crew catalogue. He admires a beautiful brunette in "buttery soft" flannel pajamas who sits under a Christmas tree with pretty packages and her handsome husband and a beatific child who is fixated on a sparkling piece of tinsel.

Next he skips to a spread titled "The Getaway," which features several shots on a sailing yacht in the Caribbean. He is taken with a lithe model wearing a bikini the catalogue refers to as "stem" but Pete recognizes as green. She has dirty blond hair and ears that are slightly too large, but excellent cheekbones and a wonderfully curved upper lip.

He fixates on a shot where she wears white Capri pants and a striped "finely ribbed cotton" crewneck T-shirt. She sits back against a teak bulkhead, her hair blowing over a brass cowling, reading a book with its title slanted just enough to be indecipherable. Her fingers are long and thin. He toys with adding her to his list of potential brides.

He did not want to be alone and this is not helping.

Lowering himself out of the hammock, he crosses to the kitchen and pours himself a glass of Johnnie Walker. It's dark out, Drink & Dial Time.

He dials up Tina, an ex-girlfriend he has not seen in over a year, and hasn't slept with for over two.

"Hello," her message says, "you've reached Tina and Harry . . ." Demoralized, Pete hangs up. He wonders if his own answering machine will ever say, "You've reached Pete *and* . . ."

He cannot remember when exactly he started feeling occasionally uncomfortable alone and certainly does not understand why, but suspects it is insidiously built into the aging process. He thinks maybe he read an article in *Details* or *Maxim* about this.

As he heads back to the hammock, his phone rings.

"Hello?"

"Hi," Winter says. "Just finished my hour in the Pleasure Booth. Want to take me to dinner?"

A Normal Happy Life

WINTER SUCKS the Penn Cove oyster off the half shell and swallows it with an abundance of horseradish and cocktail sauce. She follows this with a healthy swig of Anchor Steam.

Pete signals the waiter for two more beers. Their table is in the patio section of Campagne, next to the brightly lit fountain. He brings Winter here often because they can smoke in the patio under the heatlamps and because it is on Post Alley, close to both his loft and the Lusty.

Winter spreads salmon pâté on a cracker. She appreciates food and drink. Pete does not understand how she eats so heartily and yet stays so thin. She does not purge, as far as he knows.

"Death Cab for Cutie is playing at the Crocodile," he says. "With 764-HERO and Zeke. And I think the Model Rockets or the Makers are opening for Built to Spill at the Showbox. And maybe Alien Crime Syndicate, too."

"I've seen 'em all."

"Saltine, Minus 5, and Nevada Bachelors at ARO.space?"

"I've seen everyone in Saltine and Minus 5 a hundred times, and I've got no interest in a Seattle band that call themselves the Nevada Bachelors. What's up with that?"

"Or we could skip the shows and just go back to my place and drink and have sex."

Pete was not planning on sleeping with Winter tonight, he just wanted to hang and talk, maybe slow things down to make room for Esmé. However, Winter is wearing a red turtleneck under a black thrift-store dinner jacket and it looks great on her and he feels each oyster she swallows.

"I called because I wanted to let you know in person that I can't be having sex with you anymore," she says.

"What?"

"Sorry."

"Is this a joke?"

"No."

"What do you mean?"

"No. More. Sex." She takes a small bite of the cracker.

"Is this about the case?"

"The case? No. Why would you say that?"

"You didn't seem to think it was a good idea for me to prosecute Keith."

"I just don't think it's a good idea for *Amber*," she says. "But you're probably perfect to prosecute it if somebody has to do it."

"Meaning?"

"You can be cold, Pete."

"Cold?"

"Yeah, but it's not an insult. You just can be, or at least act like it." She takes another bite.

"So that's what this is about? You think I'm cold."

"No, that has nothing to do with it."

"What, then? What's going on?"

"Well, I've got a boyfriend now."

"What? As of when?"

"A few weeks."

"Okay." Pete says. "I don't mind."

"Neither do I," Winter says. "But he might."

"Are you serious about this? You really have a boyfriend?"

She nods as she takes another bite.

"You could have said something," he says.

"I didn't see any reason to say anything until it got serious. I mean, come on, Pete, it's not like you've been monogamous with me."

"What's he do?" Pete is thinking he is probably in a band and Pete will use this to argue that monogamy with a band member is a senseless concept.

"He's a lawyer."

"A *lawyer*? What are you doing with a lawyer?"

"*You're* a lawyer."

"Yeah, but . . . are you serious?"

"Yep." Winter holds out the cracker. "Want a bite?"

Pete shakes his head. "What's his name?"

"Why?" She finishes off the cracker, chases it with beer.

"Maybe I know him."

"If it makes you feel better, he's not as smart or as handsome or as cool as you." She smiles at Pete, but he does not smile back. "Should I add not as powerful? Would that make you feel better about this?"

"You really want to make me feel better?"

She smiles. "I don't think I should go home with you."

"Might as well do it now, before you get too serious with this guy."

"I told you. We're already there."

"How long exactly have you been seeing him?"

"About three months."

"How serious can you be after only a couple months?"

"Pete, I'm getting old. I'm twenty-five, almost twenty-six."

"Which is almost thirty."

"*Shit,* I know."

"I was joking."

"But it *is* almost thirty, and I don't want to turn thirty and find that I wasted my prime having fun, you know. I don't want to suddenly realize I'm burned out on the fun and I'm old and alone and I fuckin' blew it."

"But why *this* guy?"

"Some guys are looking to settle down and all. You can just tell. I mean, this guy is obviously looking to get married."

"Funny you should mention that, marriage."

"Funny why? Because you think marriage is a joke?"

"No, because I've been thinking about marriage."

"No you haven't."

"I haven't?"

"At least not with me." Winter looks Pete in the eye. "You would never end up with me. I know that. I've always known that. You want . . . I don't know, but this guy would *love* to end up with me. You can tell he's not someone girls pay much attention to and he's grateful I like him. He knows what I do and accepts it, though he wants me to quit, which I also want." Her voice turns uncharacteristically serious. "I just want a normal life. I want to wake up some Sunday and *not* be hungover, have breakfast with pancakes and orange juice and kids and stuff."

"Yeah?"

"Yeah, and at some point you've got to be with a person who also wants that. Someone who realistically wants to be with you in the long run—someone who will stay with you when you're old and you've lost your looks. Someone who wants you for your soul. Everyone wants to be wanted that way, don't they?"

Pete pulls out a cigarette, lights up. "When did you become so sensible?" he asks.

Winter grins. "I don't know. Are you impressed?"

Pete nods. He is.

"I used to think I was one of those people who wasn't wired right to have a normal happy life," Winter says. "But now I think I can." She pulls out her Marlboro Menthols.

Pete wonders if *he's* the one not wired to have a normal happy life. "I'm not sure there's anything normal about being happy," he says, lighting her cigarette.

"I haven't spent a lot of time around happy people," Winter says, "but I've spent a lot of time around *un*happy people, and so I figure I can do the *opposite* of what I see unhappy people doing."

Pete thinks she has a point, even though he suspects her logic is flawed.

The waiter drops off the beer and a frosted schooner glass. He pours Winter's beer into the glass, and leaves Pete a bottle.

"I wish I'd known," Pete says, picking up his beer, "that the last time we were having sex it was the last time we would be having sex."

"We fucked *every* time like it was the last time. You gotta give us that much."

He nods, looks back at her. "One more time?"

Winter shakes her head, smokes her cigarette.

Pete takes a drink of the beer, then signals the waiter. "Scotch," he mouths. Then he turns back to Winter. *Why did she have to look so good tonight? Shouldn't she have dressed down for a breakup?* "This is . . . I don't know. I don't want to end this."

"End *what*? It's not like we're in a relationship."

"Well, we were until you just dumped me." He thinks about this. "I've just been dumped." He smiles. "I'm not sure I've ever really been dumped before."

"You're not being *dumped,* and you probably never have been dumped because you always let your relationships fade out so nobody really gets dumped. You just quit calling, leave town, whatever."

"Hey, I haven't done that with you."

"Eventually you would."

"Winter . . ." He takes a long drag of his cigarette, exhales. "We have good sex, yes?"

"Yes."

"*Great* sex."

"Yes."

"And we don't fight."

"No."

"And we like hanging out together."

"Yes."

"And we *get* each other."

"Yes."

"And you're not married yet."

"No."

"So shouldn't we keep—"

"Don't do the cross-examination thing on me," she says, "where you try to trap me. Remember, I've seen you in court."

Pete still thinks he can win this argument if he plays it out hard enough.

The scotch arrives. Pete holds up the glass in a toast gesture. Winter holds up her Anchor Steam and they clink.

"Well," Pete says, "here's to your future."

"Thanks."

They drink.

"This guy hasn't asked you to marry him," Pete says, "has he?"

"Not yet. But he will."

"So when things—*if* things don't work out . . ."

"I'll probably come knocking at your door," she smiles, "lonely and horny."

"So I've got that to look forward to."

"You don't mind if I steal some of the silverware here, do you?" she asks. "I'm making him dinner and I realized I don't have any matching forks and knives and stuff."

You've Got Mail, Damn It

A MESSAGE from Scott appears on Pete's computer screen: Sundfell just called. He must realize I'm the nicer guy

Pete types back: Scott, your office is ten feet from mine. Walk down here and talk to me like a human.

A moment later another message appears: says his client won't stip to a polygraph because he doesn't trust thm

Who doesn't trust them? Pete types back. Sundfell or his client?

Scott: both

Pete: Bullshit. Sundfell uses polygraphs whenever he thinks he has someone who can pass, either someone innocent or a total sociopath

Scott: wel he's not doing one for this case

Pete: You know what that means?

Scott: keith is neither innocent nor a sociopath??

Pete: Sundfell took Keith for a test ride on a private polygraph. And he flunked.

Scott: so we've got ourselves a trial

Pete: Yep. I have a domestic and an attempted rape also set that day, but I'll clear them out with continuances or sweetheart pleas. How's your schedule look?

Scott: had a child molest 1 comin up but the perv hung himself in jail, so that helps . . .

The Decline of Western Civilization

PAYTON DRIVES past Kobe, but Shaq cuts him off. Payton zings the ball back to Detlef who sets up and sinks a three-pointer for a one-point lead with forty-two seconds left on the clock. Lakers call a twenty-second time-out.

Gary Glitter's "Rock and Roll Part II" thumps out from the Arena speakers and the crowd stays on its feet. Pete cannot remember what happened with the child pornography or sex charges Mr. Glitter was facing in England.

"Why are we still standing?" Esmé asks. "Just to see the stupid ape mascot?"

"It's a Sasquatch."

The Sasquatch and the Sonics girls clear the floor and the Lakers inbound the ball, work it to Shaq. The big man is instantly double-teamed and he cannot get a good look at the basket, so he simply runs over Vin Baker and stuffs the ball in the hole—an obvious charge, which goes uncalled. The fans boo.

"Why are they booing?" Esmé asks.

"They're booing the foul," Pete says.

"What foul?"

"The foul that wasn't called when Shaq bulldozed Baker."

"If it was a foul why wasn't it called?"

"Because Shaq is a star and he plays for L.A." Scott contributes the standard Seattle sports-fan position. "Teams like

L.A. receive preferential treatment. Seattle's still not a major media draw, other than in rock-and-roll."

Payton goes toe-to-toe with Kobe at the top of the key as the clock ticks down—ten, nine, eight—then Payton drives and Shaq moves to cut him off, but Hawkins slices into the open space and Payton paws off a quick bounce pass and Hawkins grabs it on the fly and lays it in off the backboard.

One point lead, Sonics. Time-out, Lakers.

Scott claps along with the crowd while the Ventures' "Diamond Head" plays.

"Local band," Pete says.

"Who?" Esmé asks.

"The Ventures."

"Aren't they a surf band from California?"

"Tacoma, Washington. Used to play at Bob's Java Jive. Little known Northwest rock-and-roll trivia."

"I've been there," Shannon says. "Bob's Java Jive. Cool jukebox."

The players take the floor. L.A. inbounds from half court. Rick Fox looks for Shaq, makes the pass, but Payton—"The Glove"—steals the ball and the game.

"Do people always freak out like this?" Esmé asks over the crowd noise.

"It's something about beating L.A. Good triumphing over evil and all that."

"You realize we're watching the decline of Western civilization," Esmé says. "Sports fanaticism, the frenzy over Clinton's sex life, celebrity obsession, the Columbine High School shootings, the fact that nobody has bothered to shoot the Spice Girls, all signs of a dying society."

"The Spice Girls are on my list of people to kill if I get a fatal disease," Pete assures her. "I'll do it for you."

"You've got a real romantic streak."

As they herd out with the crowd, Pete tells Esmé, "This may be the last time I can hang out for a while."

"Why?"

"Can't resolve the Keith Junior case, so I'm going to start obsessing."

"Obsessing? What do you do?"

"Oh, I read all the reports and statements about ten times each, check with all the witnesses, rehearse, and just pace around and talk to the walls."

"I might like to see that."

He shakes his head. "No."

Two guys in baseball caps are walking beside them and Pete notices that they keep glancing over.

"You Pete Tyler?" one finally asks.

Scott looks up.

"Yes," Pete says.

"Whole thing's a fucking sham, man."

"Fascist motherfucker," the other adds.

"Fucking *suit*."

"Fuck you."

"Fuck *you*."

"*Fuck you*."

"Hey," Scott says, "you Nimrods want to take this outside and elevate the dialogue?"

Esmé grabs Pete's arm. "Don't do something stupid."

The baseball cap guys both give the middle finger gesture behind their backs as they walk ahead and merge into the crowd.

"What the hell was *that* about?" Shannon says.

"The trial," Scott says. "It's about time we started getting a little publicity."

"I can't believe someone called me a 'suit.'"

"You were also called a motherfucker and a fascist," Scott points out.

"A '*suit*,'" Pete repeats.

Always Something There to Remind Me

SCOTT AND Shannon split off to find the Dodge Diplomat, which Scott apparently misplaced. Pete and Esmé continue on to the Seattle Center Fun Forest. They walk east toward the Flag Pavilion as the hoist lines clank in the wind against the towering bare poles. A light rain is falling and the drizzle shines in the lights surrounding the fountain.

They pass the carnival rides, which are lit but not running. The "Wild Storm" roller coaster has replaced the "Wild Mouse" from Pete's youth, which irritates him.

Esmé detours into a public restroom at the loading ramp for the monorail entrance. Pete notices gang graffiti on the metal sheets protecting the game booths. There was no gang graffiti when he grew up in Seattle, just teenage bulletins such as "Pete + Melinda = Love" or "Nathan Hale High Rules!" or maybe just a random "FUCK."

Esmé emerges and hands him a white cotton cloth, which he realizes, after examining, would be her panties.

"Could you put those in your pocket, please? I don't have room in my purse."

Not knowing what to make of this, he does as she requests and waits for an explanation.

"Thanks." She smiles.

Pete shrugs, then buys two tickets.

While they wait, he steps over to the edge of the ramp and looks up at the Space Needle, which is dizzying from this angle, the yellow lights of the saucer looking like something from *The X-Files.*

"Symbol of the future," Esmé says. "It was built in 1961 in preparation for the World's Fair of 1962. Six hundred and five feet tall, including the aircraft warning beacon."

"How do you know this?"

"The ride up takes exactly forty-three seconds. The structure bends one inch for every ten miles per hour of wind. The restaurant at the top makes a complete rotation in one hour and twenty minutes."

"*Why* do you know this?"

"I was an elevator operator."

The monorail pulls into the station. They approach the electric train that is vaguely reminiscent of the shuttles in *Star Trek.*

"I also know a few facts about the monorail," she says.

Pete hands their tickets to the operator in front. There is no one else on board. Bluish fluorescent lights flicker eerily as they walk down the aisle lined with plastic bench seats.

"Let's sit in back," Esmé suggests, then switches into her tour guide voice. "The monorail departs every fifteen minutes, which, incidentally, is close to the average length of intercourse for most couples, according to *Cosmo.*"

Pete takes a seat on the back bench and Esmé climbs on top, facing him.

"The length of the ride is 1.1 mile," she whispers into his ear as she unsnaps his Levi's button fly. Her hand wiggles through the opening of his boxers. "We will be traveling on a track twenty-five feet above the street level."

His eyes go to the driver, who is tapping one of the instruments in front of him.

"There are only two stops," Esmé continues. "Here, at the base of the Space Needle, and Fifth and Pine, near Nordstrom's."

His eyes go back to hers and she takes one of his fingers into her mouth and this has the effect she intends. She then puts her fingers in her own mouth and then, smiling at him, puts her hand under her skirt. She locks eyes with him and after a few moments takes him inside of her.

"The monorail can reach a top speed of seventy miles an hour," she says. "But we will only reach fifty miles an hour."

She moves her hips slowly and slightly and he responds in kind. Another couple steps inside and Pete watches over her shoulder.

"We've got company," he says, stopping his motion.

"Total capacity is four hundred and fifty," she says, continuing her motion. "But sometimes on weeknights the driver will transport a nearly empty train. Always stays on schedule."

The other couple sits near the front, keeping a comfortable distance from the man with a woman mounted on his lap.

"On an average weekend," Esmé continues, "over two thousand people will make the trip from the Space Needle to downtown." She grinds harder and faster.

Pete moves his pelvis while simultaneously trying to keep his head and shoulders steady and his expression blank. His hands move to her hips.

"Eight electric engines," Esmé says. "Seven hundred volts of electricity hum through the tracks." She begins nibbling on his ear.

The monorail pulls slowly out of the station. Pete takes the opportunity to increase his pelvic motions, exaggerating the slight bumping of the shuttle. They pass through the construction of the Experience Music Project.

"We'll reach top speed as we travel above the traffic on Fifth Avenue," Esmé says.

As they become increasingly less discreet, Pete wonders what law they are breaking.

"We're almost there," she says in his ear. "Top speed. Near the old Astor Park."

"Band played at that club a couple of times," Pete mutters.

"We're hitting top speed."

Pete glimpses the boarded-up Astor Park space as they fly by at roof level and then Esmé whispers something about the monorail's imminent arrival, and then, suddenly, she adjusts and he's out.

She tucks him back into his Levi's, which is not a simple task given his unrelieved state, and then she slides off and sits beside him.

The side doors slide open with a pneumatic hiss.

"Good luck in the trial."

"You know," he says, "I might have some free time after opening statement."

And Don't Steal the Silverware

"HI," WINTER says on her answering machine, "you can leave me a message if you don't care when I call you back, or you can page me."

"Winter," Pete says loudly, "pick up, it's an emergency."

"Pete?" she says, obviously just waking up. "What's wrong?"

"My mother just called me."

"So?"

"I need a date tonight."

She moans. "Call me back later."

"No, you have to get up and get ready."

"What are you talking about?"

"I've got this family dinner thing my mother has been planning for weeks and I have to find a date. I tried to get out of it, but I can't. I owe it to my mother."

"Why are you telling me this?"

"You're my date."

"Me? Why don't you ask that Esther girl."

"Who?"

"Or Esmé, or whatever her dumb name is. The Sub Pop girl."

"How do you know about her?"

"It's a small town, Pete."

"I can't ask her because . . . it would put too much pressure on her, but with you . . . hey, you've already dumped me so there won't be any pressure."

"You know what's funny?"

"What?"

"When I first got involved with you, I thought *I* was the crazy one."

Come As You Are

WINTER OPENS the door of her University District duplex. She is wearing a black lace slip and black gloves and Doc Martens.

"We're already late," Pete says, "throw on a dress and let's go."

"I *am* wearing a dress."

Pete stares. "That's a *slip.*"

"It *was* a slip. Now it's a dress. You want to just forget this?"

"No, no, let's go."

Pete takes Forty-fifth to Aurora Avenue, where he turns south. Canlis, a classic Seattle establishment from the 1950s, sits on the northeast slope of Queen Anne Hill near the end of the Aurora Bridge. The fifties architecture includes angled floor-to-ceiling glass walls, which look out on Lake Union and downtown. The average age of the clientele is in the sixties. The gentlemen all wear suits and ties and their wives wear pearls and, at least for an evening, here they can act like the world isn't going to hell in a handbasket.

Pete notices eyes following Winter as they pass through and he can sense the jolt of testosterone she triggers in the older men's declining systems—something atavistic inside them visibly awakens, which spooks him.

"Hope I die before I get old . . ."

Well, not really.

They arrive at his mother's window table approximately ninety minutes late, which is actually only thirty minutes late, which is exactly when Pete is expected.

Greetings are exchanged. They sit. Pete hails one of the Asian waitresses, notices that *all* the waitresses are Asian. Katie and his mother already have wine so he orders a Laphroaig and an Anchor Steam for Winter.

"And a kamikaze," Winter adds.

"Where's William?" Pete asks Katie.

"Working this weekend. Something big's going on."

"Has the coup begun?"

"He won't tell me."

"Well, he's just looking out for your safety."

"You know," Pete's mother says, "I don't get all these Microsoft jokes."

"It's okay, Mother," Pete says. "I think it's great that you know nothing about computers."

"Why should I?"

"Exactly."

"So, Winter," Pete's mother says, "how do you and Pete know each other?"

Winter glances at Pete, smiles, then turns back to his mother. "He used to come into the place I work at."

"Oh. Where's that?"

"It's called the Lusty."

Katie reacts with widened eyes.

Pete's mother, however, is apparently unfamiliar with the Lusty. "The Lusty?" she says.

"It's what they call a peep show," Winter says. "Except with live girls. Like that old Madonna video."

"Across from the Seattle Art Museum," Katie helps out.

"Oh, yes."

Pete looks like he's been poleaxed. He just assumed Winter would lie about her occupation if it came up.

"They have the marquee with all the clever puns and so forth," Katie continues.

"Right."

Pete turns his attention to Lake Union, which is speckled with sailboats taking advantage of a stiff evening wind. A Union Air floatplane takes off heading north, probably to Roche Harbor in the San Juan Islands, or Bedwell Harbor in the Canadian Gulf Islands. Pete would like to be on that plane.

"We met in the Pleasure Booth," Winter decides to explain, "this room where the dancers can talk to the customers. You're separated by a glass wall but there are these phones you can talk on." Winter's tongue stud clicks. "He's the only guy I've ever met there that I ended up going out with."

"Really," Pete's mother says. She turns to Pete.

"The only one," he says.

The drinks arrive. Pete takes a long guzzle of his scotch. Winter takes the kamikaze down in one gulp, then sips from her beer.

"I should check on William and William Jr.," Katie says, standing.

"They recently installed a phone in the ladies' room," Mother informs her.

"Winter?" Katie says.

"Yeah, I should probably go, too," Winter says. "I could use a cigarette."

Pete and his mother look at each other for several beats, Pete partially hiding behind his drink.

"Winter is very pretty," his mother offers.

"Yes, she is."

"Her makeup is a little severe, however."

"I think it works on her."

"And what is this new style with all the earrings and nose thing and so forth?"

Pete shrugs. "You got me."

"But I can see how you two would get along."

"You *can*?"

"Sure. She seems like she could challenge you, Peter, and you need that."

Yeah, it's a challenge having sex two or three times a night when you're almost forty.

"If you love her and end up with her, well, you have my total support. I'm your mother."

Anything Goes

THE TITLE track of Social Distortion's *Prison Bound* plays on Pete's Sony Walkman. He clicks it off and removes the headphones when he sees Trish, the judicial assistant, open the jury room door. He and Scott stand as twelve jurors and one alternate are ushered into the box. Three days were spent selecting these thirteen, but they could all be concealing criminal insanity as far as Pete knows.

Judge Sorensen, gray-haired and black-robed, also stands. To his left is the American flag, and to his right is the green flag of Washington State. Daylight filters through stained-glass windows at the top of the dark oak-paneled walls. Pete feels the same reverence in here that he felt in church as a child.

The jurors position themselves in front of their assigned seats. As the judge swears them in, Pete glances at the gallery. A few reporters are in back, but Judge Sorensen did not allow any cameras. Per tradition, the defendant's supporters sit behind Sundfell and the firm's newest junior associate, Sue Naomi, a.k.a. Satan's Little Helper, whose main job is to wear short skirts and sit next to the defendant and humanize him by periodically touching his shoulder and whispering in his ear.

Keith Junior is wearing tan pants and a blue cotton shirt, something he probably has not worn since grammar school. His supporters, however, are dressed in their usual garb and look

like a *Rocky Horror Picture Show* crowd. Pete recognizes various faces from his past and it feels odd to see them lined up
against him.

Behind Pete and Scott, by contrast, there are only four people.
Amber and her closest friends are not allowed in until closing argument because they are witnesses, so it is just two prosecutors
from the Misdemeanor Division who are there to watch Pete's
opening or to check out the girls on Keith's side, and Esmé, who
is in the front row, and Winter, who is sitting on the edge of the
prosecution side in the far back, just across the aisle from friends
of Keith's.

Pete suddenly hears the judge say his name, followed by,
"who will be giving opening statement on behalf of the state."
His cue.

Pete has been stressed and isolated in trial mode for the past
week, but he feels it all wash away now in a rush of pretrial anticipation. He has the usual anticipatory tightness, the uncomfortable yet welcome buzz he has sought in different forms for
many years.

He steps toward the jury, stops a few feet away. "This is a case
about what happens when anything goes." *Anything goes.* Pete
plans to repeat Winter's phrase at least ten times in opening,
using it to describe a code of conduct, the defendant's world-
view.

The best story usually wins in the courtroom. Not necessarily
the truest story, but the most believable story, the story the jurors want to buy, the one that engages them and moves them
and makes them want to do something to set things right, or so
Pete trusts.

He starts off by introducing Amber, telling how she graduated
from a small high school in eastern Washington, moved to Seattle, found a barely affordable studio apartment, got a job, met
people, made friends, tried to start a life. Once he has estab-
lished her as a sympathetic character, he moves to the night of
the incident, progressing chronologically, telling everything
from Amber's point of view. He is especially unemotional when

he comes to the most wrenching moments because he has found that jurors, particularly women, will therefore take it upon themselves to express the emotion that he is not, and three or four of them do so when he gets to the point where Amber is cowering in the bathroom with her back to the door and her legs braced up against the toilet.

"And then he knocks on the door. Her body jolts. She's scared, panicked, confused. She's eighteen and in awe of this guy. He's not some stranger in a parking garage with a knife. He's a guitarist for a well-known local band. She thought he was cool. She thought she was safe. She trusted him. And he raped her. But now he's outside the bathroom door acting like it's not that big of a deal. 'Not very cool of me,' he says.

"She eventually lets him in, because what else is she going to do? She's never been in a situation like this and has no idea what to do. He takes control and talks her back into bed. She's afraid, doesn't want a confrontation. She decides she'll leave as soon as he falls asleep. But she passes out.

"When she wakes up, it's still dark and he's still asleep. So she quickly escapes. As she walks home in the rain she feels *sick*. Amber will tell you that she actually felt like she was 'shrinking and withering away.' "

Pete will have to remind her to use those words as she did in an interview.

He knows Sundfell's likely opening theme is regret, that Amber regrets having sex with the defendant and is therefore now calling it rape; so after he describes the reporting sequence and the invasive rape exam, he wraps up with a riff on regret.

"Amber regrets this night. She regrets drinking, she regrets going back to the defendant's place, she regrets kissing him, but these are not things she would normally regret. She regrets these things on this night for one reason: she was raped."

Pete loses awareness of the gallery when he's addressing the jury, but when he finishes and is stepping back to counsel table he sees the women behind Keith Junior, and their expressions have changed, hardened into wonder and concern. Pete can always tell how well his opening went by how stressed the defendant's supporters appear.

"Mr. Sundfell," Judge Sorensen says.

Sue's hand is on Keith's shoulder and she appears to be whispering in his ear, per the standard script. Sue recently left her husband, a batterer, and Pete wonders if she's sleeping with Sundfell, assumes he beats her.

"Thank you, Your Honor," Sundfell says. "I'll waive opening at this time and just ask that the jury keep an open mind."

Sad Movies

PETE IS quiet as he and Esmé walk out of the downtown Cineplex Odeon after watching *Saving Private Ryan*. He is thinking his own generation is a bunch of sissies.

Judge Sorensen had adjourned court early, and, unlike in the movies and on TV, there was no horde of camera-armed journalists waiting to ambush Pete. Still, he left the building just in case.

"What's the difference between Clinton and the *Titanic*?" Esmé asks.

"Only five hundred women went down on the *Titanic*."

They exit onto Seventh Avenue just as the workday is ending for most people and Pete likes the feeling of playing hookey. The rush-hour foot traffic includes a variety of women in their skirts, nylons, heels, scarves, and fluttering overcoats.

"Could you tone it down a little?" Esmé says.

"What?"

"That last one wasn't even good looking."

"Just checking out the fashions."

"A sudden interest in fashion? I've never seen you wear anything but white shirts and blue suits."

"I like fashion, just not on myself."

Pete lights a cigarette as they turn west on Pike. A blood-red glow spreads on the horizon as the sun sets behind a thin layer of cirrus clouds.

Another goddam sunset.

"Thanks for coming to see opening," Pete says. "I felt out-numbered, and it was good to see you."

"You seemed like a real grown-up in front of the jury."

"So you think I fooled 'em?"

"Even fooled me for a second or two."

They stop at the corner in front of Eddie Bauer to wait for the light. Esmé's hair flies around in the swirling wind and her cheeks are red and Pete notices how good she looks in this light.

"I'm giving up my place at the end of the month," she says.

"What?"

"Would you quit with the 'what' stuff?"

"I just said 'what' because I don't see why you would give up your apartment."

"I told you. I'm supposed to go to law school."

"But that's not until fall, is it?"

"Orientation and all that starts in August, and I want to look for a place to live in New Haven. It's not the best area, I hear."

"Still, you've got almost three months."

"But I need to move in with my parents to save money in the meantime."

"You're really going to law school?"

"I guess so."

"You don't sound very definite."

"I'm not."

The white WALK light comes on and they cross Fifth Avenue toward Rainier Square. As they do, a girl begins waving franti-cally from the Pine Street crosswalk: Gina the Faith-Healing Waitress of Unknown Age, who looks like she just finished her shift.

Pete waves back. *Please don't come say hello.*

"Who's that?" Esmé asks.

"Waitress."

"Did you go out with her?"

"She's engaged. She may even be married by now."

"But did you go out with her?"

"No." Pete picks up the walking pace, putting distance between them and Gina.

"So you just slept with her?"

"Well, yes."

Esmé glances over again. "Little young, isn't she?"

"Whatever you decide to do," he says, "you shouldn't move back in with your parents."

"Why not? Free rent."

"I tried that once. When the band broke up, I moved back in with my parents. My mother was cooking me these great meals and everything, but . . . it doesn't work." He puts Beth out of his mind. "There are all these things around from your childhood and adolescence. It's not healthy."

They pass the old Brooks Brothers location, now filled by a Tully's coffee shop.

He adds, "And you'll miss being in Seattle."

"I will, but I don't know," she says. "I'm getting kind of old for the nightlife thing."

What does that make me?

"Okay," he says. "But don't move in with your parents. What if you decide you don't want to go to law school and you have to start apartment hunting again? It's hell finding an apartment in Seattle these days."

"But I *am* going to go to law school."

"Wait, I thought you just said you weren't definite."

"I'm *probably* going to go."

"Doesn't it make sense to keep your apartment until you're sure? What if you decide to go to UW instead of Yale?"

"If I'm going to do it, I'm going to do it all the way. Why go to UW when I've been accepted at Yale?"

Pete hesitates on this one. They reach Third Avenue and slalom around the orange traffic cones, by-products of the endless street construction.

"What do you think about this, Pete?"

"What?"

"*Stop* that."

"I'm serious. What do I think about what?"

"What do you think I should do?"

"I told you."

"But I didn't hear you suggesting anything."

"I suggested you keep your apartment."

She mutters something.

"Rents are out of control," he continues. "Hold on to what you have."

"But what if I leave?"

"I don't know."

They take a right on University and head down the hill.

"Where are we going?" she suddenly asks.

Pete wonders if she means this literally or metaphorically.

"My place," he says.

"Why?"

Oh, Jesus. "What do you mean?"

"What's the point?"

"What's *that* mean?"

"Aren't you fucking *listening*. I . . . am . . . leaving."

Pete drops his cigarette. "Okay, we've gone from *not definite* to *probably* to *done deal?*"

"Why *shouldn't* I go? You know what I'm saying. Do I have to spell it out any more obviously?"

Pete stops to light another Camel. Esmé keeps walking. He catches up to her in a few feet. "You know, I don't think this is something that needs to be decided right now."

"I've been wanting to discuss it with you for the past couple weeks but you've been wrapped up in the trial."

"And I still am. All I wanted was to relax with you today. I've got a lot going on now—too *much* going on—and I just can't deal with anything intense or long-term right now."

"I've got a feeling there's *never* a time when you want to deal with something intense and long-term."

"I don't want to get into this now."

Esmé pauses, then says, "What do you think will happen with us if I move to New Haven?"

"Realistically?"

"Sure," she says, "realistically."

Coming into view ahead is the red neon Pike Place Market sign with the big clock standing out against the darkening orange of the sunset.

Goddam clock.

"I don't know," he says. "At first, we'll talk every night on the phone, then it will be every couple nights, then it will be once a week, then we'll just start exchanging the occasional e-mail—"

"Okay, okay, I've had about enough realism, thank you." She turns and raises her hand for a taxi, though there are not any in sight.

"Now what?" he says.

Esmé keeps her attention focused on the street.

Pete knows this sensation—once again he has fucked up a relationship without even trying, or even understanding.

"Come on," he says.

"This is pointless."

"What?"

A STITA taxi rounds the corner and Esmé steps out into the street further than necessary, which appears to alarm the turban-wearing cabbie, who quickly stops. Esmé swings open the back door.

"Where are you going?"

She climbs in. "Oh, and I know you've been seeing other women, including the one who was watching the trial this morning."

Pause.

"I never said I wasn't!"

"Yeah, but I want you to know I know!" She slams the door.

Pete watches the cab merge into the jammed traffic. He could probably catch up at a fast jog.

Instead, he turns and walks down University toward the fifty-foot scrap-metal sculpture of *Hammering Man* at the Seattle Art Museum entrance. Across First Avenue the Lusty marquee reads:

SPRING IS HERE

AND LOVE IS IN THE BARE

Showtime

"FEELING OKAY?"

Amber nods. She looks pale and not okay.

Pete sits down next to her on a hallway bench he has shared with dozens of victims. "The jury is going to like you," he says.

"My stomach is all fucked up."

"You *look* good, though."

She is wearing no makeup and a dark blue skirt and a light blue blouse, Pete's suggestions, and black tights and a Saint Christopher on a short chain, her choices.

"They're going to like you," he repeats. "And they're going to know you're telling the truth."

"I'm going to be under oath, right?"

"Right."

"I think I should tell you something."

Oh, no. "Yes?"

"I don't really remember if I screamed or not. I *think* I did, it seems like I would, but I'm not sure."

"That's okay. Just tell the jury you think you did but you're not sure."

"And I drank a little more than I first said."

"That's okay. We don't have to get into exact numbers."

"And I vomited at the Breakroom."

"That's okay."

"And there were drugs."

"What? What drugs?" *Oh, fuck, please let it be marijuana.*

"Heroin."

"Oh, *fuck.*"

"You're mad."

"Heroin?"

"But just nasal. No needle."

"How much?"

"Another girl and I bought a gram and I just did a bump."

"Who had the bindle?"

"She did, and she left with some guy, so I didn't see her again that night."

"Okay. Okay. I'm going to have to ask you about this on the stand."

"I know."

"I'm also going to have to ask why you didn't tell the detective about this."

"It's pretty obvious, isn't it?"

"And why you didn't tell the defense attorney when he interviewed you."

"Is he going to give me a hard time about this?"

Pete nods. "Oh, yeah."

"He didn't seem that evil when he interviewed me."

"Tactical choice. He was probably holding back so he could catch you off guard in front of the jury."

Amber buries her head in her palms. "How did I get myself into this?"

"You were raped."

"I've got to quit doing stuff like that, getting wasted and going home with guys like that and . . . stupid, stupid, stupid shit."

"Amber?"

She lifts her head back up.

"Who do you prefer," he asks, "Nirvana or Pearl Jam?"

Her face transforms. "Nirvana, I guess."

"Thought so."

"Why?"

"No reason. Just wanted to change the subject because we're about to go on. You ready?"

She nods.

"I'm going to start by asking your address."

"I think I can handle that."

"And you're not going to get emotional on me."

"Not when you ask my address."

He smiles. "Good. Let's go."

"There's no way to avoid this?"

"He could break down and plead guilty as soon as we walk into the courtroom, but I wouldn't bet on it."

Regret

TEARS ARE streaming down Amber's face by the time Pete finishes his direct examination, just as he had hoped, and she is not the only one in the courtroom sniffling.

Pete hands Amber a tissue. "No further questions," he says, then looks at Sundfell. *Have fun dealing with this, Mr. Sleaze.*

Sundfell steps tentatively toward the witness, sets his trial notebook on the wooden railing. He surprises Pete by starting off slow with simple, nonhostile questions. When Amber's tears are entirely dry he moves to the incident.

"You remember Keith looking for a condom?"

"He got off me, if that's what you mean."

"And that's when you went to the bathroom?"

"Yes."

"And closed the door and locked it."

"Yes."

"And he didn't try to break it down or anything."

She shakes her head.

"You'll have to speak up for the court reporter, please."

"No," she says. "I don't think he tried to break down the door."

"And you let him into the bathroom after a while."

"Yes."

"And he didn't attack you or anything at that point."

"No."

"He just used the bathroom."

"Yes."

"You didn't run out of the apartment or anything."

"No. I didn't know what to do. I just—"

She appears to be on the verge of tears and Sundfell cuts her off, but with a softer tone. "You went to bed."

"Yeah."

"And you ended up passing out."

"Yeah."

"You had several beers earlier at the Breakroom."

"Yes."

"And some more beer at Keith's house."

"Yes."

"And some Jack Daniel's at Keith's house."

"Right."

"And heroin at the Breakroom."

She nods.

"Yes?" Sundfell says.

"Yes."

"And you didn't tell the detective about the heroin."

"No."

"And you didn't tell me about the heroin when I interviewed you."

"No."

"In fact, I specifically asked you if you had done any drugs that night."

"Yeah, I think you asked that."

"And you said no."

"Right."

"Which was a lie."

"Right. I already admitted that when Mr. Tyler was asking me questions."

"So you lied about that."

"Objection—asked and answered."

"Sustained."

"You bought the heroin from a guy named Chino, didn't you?"

"Yes."

Fucking Sundfell has known about this for weeks.

"And you bought a full gram."

"Yes."

"So you had several beers, a few shots of Jack Daniel's, and some heroin on this night."

"Yes."

"So your memory of this night is a little fuzzy."

"About some things."

"Like, for example, whether or not you screamed."

"Yeah."

"Would you agree with me that beer, Jack Daniel's, and heroin, all combined, might affect a person's perception?"

"Somewhat, yeah."

"You don't weigh much, do you?"

"No."

"About one hundred and twenty?"

"One hundred and ten."

"And I believe you testified that you don't generally drink a lot."

"No, no I don't."

"And you've only done heroin a few times."

"Yeah."

"So the alcohol and drugs hit you pretty hard that night."

"I suppose."

"You suppose?"

"Yes."

"And would you agree with me that someone who has been drinking and doing drugs might do some things she wouldn't do if she *wasn't* drinking and doing drugs?"

"Objection," Pete says, since Sundfell is killing her. "Asks for speculation."

"I'll rephrase," Sundfell says, momentarily flashing to the jury his innate nastiness. "Have *you* done things when you've been drinking and on drugs that you might not have otherwise done?"

"Yes."

"And regretted those things when you sobered up?"

"Yes."

"So you know about those mornings where you're not sure what you did the night before but you just feel this regret and vague anger and want to lash out."

"Objection," Pete says.

"Sustained."

Sundfell turns a page in his trial notebook.

Scott whispers to Pete. "Regret and vague anger? Sounds like a typical Saturday morning for me."

Sundfell stands there for a couple more beats, turns another page, then closes the notebook.

He looks at Amber, she stares back, and it is ugly.

"No further questions."

"Mr. Tyler?" Judge Sorensen says.

Pete looks at Amber and he wants to do something for her. *Quit while we're behind.*

"Thank you, Your Honor, nothing further."

A Priest Named Pat

"JESUS DIED for somebody's sins, but not mine . . ."
The Patti Smith opening to "Gloria" echoes in Pete's head as
he enters St. James and crosses himself. He pushes the lyric out
of mind as he steps into the darkness of the long room.
Life-sized paintings along the walls chart the passion of Jesus
frame by frame, from his betrayal to his crucifixion to his resurrection. Pete must have spent hundreds of hours of his youth
staring at this story, wondering if it were true, feeling guilty for
his skepticism.

Pete has not been to church in nearly twenty years and he feels
chills. He is surprised to find the power of awe is there for him
now just as it was when he was an easily spooked adolescent.

"Can I help you?"

Pete turns to see a priest who appears younger than himself.

"I was thinking of, well, maybe spending some time in the confessional."

Priest Boy nods and turns. Pete, after hesitating, follows.
Priest Boy does not look back before stepping into his side of the
confessional.

Pete considers bolting, then sucks it up, enters. The room is
even smaller and darker than Pete remembers, and the un-
padded seat even more uncomfortable.

Pete crosses himself and says, "Forgive me, Father, for I have
sinned."

"How long since your last confession?"

"About twenty years."

"Twenty years?"

"About."

"Why so long?"

"My parents told me that after I turned sixteen, attending church would be my own choice. So I quit."

"And why are you back?"

"I was here for the Easter service with my mother."

"But why are you *here,* with me?"

"First I have to ask you something."

"Yes?"

"How old are you?"

"Twenty-eight."

"I've gotta tell you, I'm not comfortable calling someone younger than myself Father."

"I understand. Would you prefer to call me Pat?"

Pete tries out the sound. "Forgive me, Pat, for I have sinned." *Oh, God.* "No. That doesn't work. I'll stick with Father."

"What can I help you with?"

"I'm worried about the future."

"Yes?"

"Well, I've had sex with about three hundred women, give or take. I can hardly even look at a woman without wondering what she would be like in bed."

"Three hundred?"

"If you average it out, it's only about fifteen a year."

"You believe you've had sex with three hundred women?"

"Counting blow jobs."

"Sounds like you've had an unusually high amount of sexual encounters for someone who's never been elected to public office."

"Hey, that was pretty funny."

"I've found that humor helps sometimes. Have you really had sex with that many women?"

"I was in a band," Pete explains.

"Did you find sex with this many women to be a satisfying experience?"

"Mostly," Pete says, "yes."

"Did you love these women?"

"I think so, maybe. A few of them."

"And the others?"

"I liked most of them."

"There were some you did not like?"

"Some of them I didn't get to know well enough to know if I liked them or not."

"And didn't you find this unsatisfying?"

"Hey, I'm a guy—I enjoyed myself."

"But I assume something's changed now."

Pete nods, then says, "Yes."

"What?"

"I'm going to get married—but don't ask to whom because I don't know yet."

Priest Boy is mercifully silent.

"I've met this woman," Pete continues, "and I'm worried I may be falling in love with her. But there's two others I don't think I'm over. One of them I never even pictured as a possible wife until she dumped me. The other is my first love and I haven't seen her in ten years. And maybe I'm going to fall in love with someone I haven't even met yet."

Pause.

"And everything seems to be converging at the worst possible time," he adds.

"This is difficult," Priest Boy finally says.

"What would you say love is?"

"As Tolstoy said, 'So many men, so many minds, so many hearts, so many kinds of love.' "

"You priests tend to be pretty literate, don't you?"

"The point I'm making is that love has many definitions and I can't tell you if you're in love. Nobody can."

"Okay. Worst-case scenario. Let's assume I'm in love."

"Okay."

"And let's assume I marry her. What if I cannot be monogamous? Every time I see a good-looking woman, I want her. What if that doesn't change?"

"It may not change."

"Oh, God . . ." *Whoops.* "It's just that I see a good-looking woman, sometimes even just an okay-looking woman—they've *all* got something that's appealing, some feature that's sexy—and it gives me a rush. Suddenly life is good. And I can't help but think how *great* it would be, how *heavenly* it would be, to have sex with her."

"It's not a sin to wonder."

"But what if I don't just wonder? What if I'm married and I see another woman and have to have her, and then have her. That's adultery."

"Yes."

"And that's a sin."

"Yes."

"What if it's just, say, a blow job."

"Oral sex constitutes sexual relations."

"Not according to the president of the United States, who is, after all, the leader of the free world."

"It was not moral strength that allowed him to rise to that position."

"I was afraid that was where we were going to end up."

"Where have we ended up?"

"I'm a hopeless sinner."

"You are not hopeless. Aren't there some temptations you have resisted in your life?"

Pete thinks. "I'm attracted to a couple of women I work with—actually I guess it's three, maybe four—but I haven't done anything."

"And the reason?"

"They're engaged or married, and I work with them."

"So you have some self-control. Can you think of any other examples?"

"I can work eighteen-hour days."

"So you do have some self-discipline."

"I'm just obsessive."

"Well, that can be constructive, sometimes."

"Have you seen *Trainspotting?*"

"Yes."

"I love that scene where he's reaching for the suppositories in the toilet and he climbs in and suddenly he's swimming." Pete gestures with his hands, then stops. "But anyway, what got to me was that the hero really just wanted a normal life. At first I thought the ending was facetious or ironic, since that's the requisite hip tone these days, but after a couple more viewings I realized he meant it. He really did just want a normal life. Don't you think?"

"Yes. He is clumsily aspiring to a less insane, more philosophic existence. But it has to be earned."

"Earned?"

"As Wordsworth said, 'Nothing can bring back the hour, of splendor in the grass, of glory in the flower, but we will grieve not.' " Priest Boy recites this quite well, in Pete's opinion. " 'Rather find strength in what remains behind, in the soothing thoughts that spring out of human suffering, in the faith that looks through death, in years that bring the philosophic mind.' "

Pete has a sudden image of Priest Boy, alone in his dreary little room, finding consolation in the Bible and poetry and red wine. Pete admires this, but doubts he could likewise find peace of mind. Every time he reads a good book he feels the urge to drink, smoke, chase women, *live*.

"No man ever *wants* to be monogamous," Pete suddenly says, "does he?"

"Yes, some do. And you might someday, too."

Pete wants to believe this, but cannot shake off the doubt. "And celibacy," Pete says. "How is that even possible? I don't get how you guys can be celibate."

"It's a *sacrifice*. It's *supposed* to be a sacrifice."

"Still."

"And I think it would help you."

"What? *Celibacy?*"

"A sacrifice."

"A sacrifice of what?" Pete sounds suspicious.

"Something you want, you give it up. It's a way of reminding yourself that you can't just take everything you want. You can prove self-discipline to yourself. This is the stuff of adulthood. Much good follows from such acts."

Pete would have preferred a couple dozen Hail Marys.

"Do I have to decide right now?" Pete asks. "What to give up?"

"No, you decide what and when."

Pete exhales loudly. "Okay."

"Okay."

"One last thing, though."

"Yes?"

"And this is actually the big thing."

"Yes?"

"I'm a prosecuting attorney."

"Yes?"

"And what you've heard today, well, that's just the tip of the iceberg when it comes to my sins."

"Is there something else you want to atone for?"

"Nothing in particular, but sometimes I feel like a fraud. Right now, I'm prosecuting a guy for what amounts to date rape without the date. That's what I was referring to when I said everything was converging at the worst time."

"I know. I realize who you are."

Jesus H. Christ. "What do you mean?"

"How many other prosecutors who used to be in a grunge band are prosecuting front-page rape cases this month?"

Pause.

"I didn't mean to suggest I've ever date-raped a girl," Pete says. "I haven't."

"I didn't assume you had."

"I haven't."

"Okay."

"But I've been in some gray areas. I keep thinking about that quote from Jesus, 'Let him who has not sinned cast the first stone.' Truth is, I've sinned until the cows come home and I'm casting stones anyway."

"The important thing is to recognize your sins, acknowledge

them, atone for them, and then try to lead a good life. Seek for-
giveness, and be forgiving. Remember, punishment and forgive-
ness are not incompatible. And sometimes both are needed.
Humans will always make mistakes, and there will always be a
price for our mistakes. And we *need* to pay. This is where sacrifices can come in. The way you move forward with a good life is
to pay the costs, make the sacrifices. That's how we put things
behind. That's how we feel reborn."

Ahhh, Catholicism. "Okay."

"I hope your return to the Church will be ongoing."

"It's possible," Pete says, trying to avoid both commitment
and a blatant lie.

Lust Rain Over Me

PETE WALKS out of St. James and into the light of a partially sunny day, feeling vaguely redeemed. He suspects the mood is undeserved, but enjoys it nonetheless.

He stops, catches a whiff of the blooming cherry trees, then starts hiking. Though he enjoys walking, one eye is always checking the sky for nimbus clouds.

Spring is a tease in Seattle. It appears and warms you and then it's gone, leaving you cold and wet, but with the flirtatious promise that it will someday return. Pete is mindful of this because the broken clouds are obscuring the sun with increasing frequency and the wind is starting to chill. The first raindrops hit him as he crosses the south end of the Westlake Triangle, where the skater boys perform for the tattooed girls. Pete begins looking for a taxi as he is wearing a lightweight wool suit he does not want soaked.

Then, suddenly, in his peripheral vision, he spots a girl running up Fourth Avenue with a red umbrella—she's thin and tall and dark-haired and he can see the white of her teeth from fifty feet.

World-class beauty, and great ankles.

He freezes, stares. She looks somehow familiar. He thinks maybe he met her once at a Rangehoods show at the Swiss— *Megan Stra . . . something*—but he failed to pick her up.

Did you at least try?

A Metro bus pulls into his visual frame and he loses her. He keeps his eye on the bus, though. Through the rain-streaked windows he sees her as she steps up inside and flashes a pass and takes a seat near the front.

Still frozen, he wills her to look his way.

Why didn't you get her phone number when you had the chance?

The bus pulls out. She keeps looking forward. Then suddenly she swings her head for no apparent reason and she's looking in his direction for a second, maybe.

An image of himself from her point of view comes to him: tall guy in blue suit and white shirt, handsome enough, but without the sense to come in out of the rain.

Animal House vs. Rashomon

"IT'S LIKE a scene in *Animal House*," Scott says to the jury in closing argument, and Pete blanches. "There's this character named Flounder," Scott continues, "and he's upset because the guys have trashed his brother's Lincoln Continental. Otter turns to him and says, 'Hey, you screwed up—you trusted us.' Though 'screwed up' is not the actual phrase."

There are a couple smiles of recognition from the jurors, to Pete's relief.

"That's what happened here," Scott continues. "Amber screwed up. She trusted the defendant. She made other mistakes, too. She drank too much, she did some heroin, she went home with a guy who thinks anything goes."

Watching Scott, Pete discovers, is disconcertingly like watching himself, albeit a more cavalier version, and he realizes it is because Scott has ripped him off, just as Pete ripped off other prosecutors such as Horne. Pete cannot remember if it was T. S. Eliot or John Lennon who said true artists don't plagiarize, they steal.

"There may be some things that Amber is fuzzy on, there may be some things she doesn't remember, there may be some things she doesn't know, but she *does* know she was raped. That's the kind of thing you tend to remember."

Pete moves his hand over his mouth so he will appear contemplative rather than amused.

Scott goes over the facts, then ties the facts to the jury instructions, which are typed out in large letters on poster boards. Scott explains that Rape 2 means "forcible compulsion," which is "force that overcomes resistance," and he goes back to the facts, Amber wiggling and kicking and hitting and scratching. Then Scott moves on to the lesser included offense, Rape 3, which just requires that "lack of consent was clearly communicated." He stops and looks at the jury. "Amber did a lot more than clearly communicate here. Maybe she screamed, maybe she didn't, but even if you think she didn't scream, her actions clearly communicated a lack of consent, and, more than that, her actions were resistance, which was overcome with force, which makes this Rape in the second degree. But it's also Rape in the Third Degree because lack of consent does not have to be verbal. It can be physical."

This argument gives the jury a compromise position, Rape 3, which is not entirely logical, but Pete thinks it's a smart move under the circumstances.

"Just use your common sense when you're going over the jury instructions. Use your common sense when you're going over the facts. Use your common sense when you're considering what the defendant told Detective Tuiaia. He claims he was so drunk he couldn't find any of the more than thirty condoms in the place? Come on. This guy has *never* been so drunk he couldn't find a condom."

"Objection, the prosecutor is being improper and, uh—" Sundfell sputters out on his own.

"Overruled. This is argument."

"And use your common sense when you consider Amber's testimony," Scott continues. "You heard her roommate whom she described this to. You heard the rape counselor whom she described it to. You heard from the doctor who did the rape exam. Amber has been consistent.

"Does it sound to you like she's just a girl who regrets a few too many Budweisers and a little smack? Does it sound to you like she is just a girl who is overreacting to a hangover? Do you think she is *totally insane*? Because you would have to be totally insane to make all this up. There's no reason for her to go through all this—the rape exam, the interviews, the trial—no reason to go through all this unless she was raped."

Scott spins a few more facts and then wraps it up. "This is not a case about what Amber did, it's a case about what the defendant did. This is not a case about regret, it's a case about rape. "Thank you."

Sundfell stands up and says, "What Mr. Tyler described to you in opening statement, that was rape. What Mr. Foss just described to you, that was rape. And what Ms. Nickerson described when she testified, that was rape.

"But Mr. Tyler doesn't know what happened that night. And Mr. Foss doesn't know what happened that night. And *I* don't know what happened that night. *And neither does Amber Nickerson.* She was drinking beer and Jack Daniel's for several hours, more than ten drinks, maybe even more than that, and she's not a large person. You saw her. She's thin as a reed. And she was doing heroin that night. So she really isn't sure what happened. She's even admitted that she has *lied* about what happened—she lied when she said she didn't do any drugs. Amber Nickerson simply is not to be believed. She was drunk, she was high, and she's lied. Remember, she was using fake I.D. that night.

"I'm not going to try to tell you what happened that night, because I don't know. Nobody knows. Not even Amber and Keith know for sure, because they were both *wasted.* The sex may have gotten a little rough, but that doesn't make it rape.

"Does Amber really *think* she was raped? Maybe. But she didn't report a rape to the police until *after* she talked to her roommate and a rape counselor. Maybe they talked her into believing she was raped. We don't know."

Sundfell goes on a tangent about the difficulties of knowing anything, even works in a reference to the Akira Kurosawa movie *Rashomon,* which elicits not a single flicker of recognition from the jurors, but he regains his focus. "What I know is this: it would be a mistake to convict Keith, because there are too many reasonable doubts here. There are *so many.* There's the fact that Amber was drunk and high, and the fact that she lied, and the fact that she's uncertain about screaming, and the fact that no neighbors heard any screams, and the fact that she went there voluntarily, took off her clothes voluntarily, and she admits that Keith agreed to put on a condom, and she admits she spent the night with him. She didn't decide to claim she was raped until about twenty hours later. These are all reasons to doubt. If she was raped, she would have been out of that apartment and talking to the police *that night*. But she didn't decide to call it rape until after she talked to her roommate and the rape counselor and who knows who else.

"Now, Mr. Tyler gets a last chance to talk to you because the state has the burden of proof. Mr. Tyler is going to sound persuasive. He's articulate, charming, and he tells a good story."

Scott coughs.

"But I'd ask you to keep in mind that Mr. Tyler wasn't there that night, he doesn't know what happened. None of us know what happened, and none of us ever will. *We just don't know—* it can't be known."

"Objection," Scott says.

Sundfell, the judge, and Pete all turn to Scott.

"Withdrawn," Scott says. Then he whispers to Pete, "Just fucking with him."

Sundfell picks it back up, "This case cannot be proved beyond a reasonable doubt, and so I am asking you for the only possible verdict. Two words: not guilty. Thank you."

"We'll take a fifteen-minute recess," Judge Sorensen announces, "and then we will conclude with Mr. Tyler's rebuttal argument."

Give the Devil His Due

THE COURTROOM clears except for Pete and Scott. Pete stares at his rebuttal argument, written out in double-spaced sixteen-point type.

"Want to take a cigarette break?" Scott finally asks.

"I'm trying to quit, remember?"

"I haven't noticed you trying too hard."

"Well, I'm going to start."

Pete wads up his rebuttal and tosses it in the wastebasket.

"What the hell?"

"I thought he was going to go with regret as a theme."

Scott shrugs. "Yeah, me too. But I kind of liked the switch to the nothing-is-knowable theme. Almost existential."

"And it was working, wasn't it?"

"Afraid so. And he complimented you. He's feeling cocky."

Pete looks up at the clock and then walks over to the empty jury box and begins silently rehearsing a new rebuttal argument.

Scott says, "I think you should throw in a Clinton joke."

Truth Is Beauty

"DEFENSE COUNSEL would have you believe that nothing is knowable," Pete says as he approaches the jury, "that we can't know the truth, so we might as well not try to achieve justice." He stops. "But we *can* know things, we *can* recognize the truth, and we *can* achieve justice. That's exactly what we're here to do."

Pete crosses to the table in front of the judicial assistant with the exhibits and picks up plaintiff's exhibit number 16, Amber's underwear, in a clear plastic bag.

"We know Amber's underwear is torn." He holds it up to the jury for several beats, then sets it down and picks up plaintiff's exhibit number 3, a photo of the defendant taken at the jail.

"We know the defendant looked like he had been hit in the face the way Amber described." He sets down that photo and picks up exhibit number 4, another photo.

"We know Amber's legs were bruised. You can see marks that look like finger pressure points." He sets this down and picks up plaintiff's exhibit number 6, two twelve-packs of Trojans, a three-pack of Natural X in blue plastic capsules, and several other Natural X's in the traditional foil pack.

"We know the defendant's house was chock full of condoms, most of these in plain sight near the bed, so we know the defendant's claim that they didn't have intercourse because he thought he was out of condoms doesn't ring true." He sets down the condoms, looks at Sundfell, then back to the jury. "Come on. We're all intelligent people here. We can figure things out."

Be easier, though, if the taped semi-confession hadn't been suppressed.

He steps away from the exhibits and back to center stage. "What happened here is the defendant was out of control, he was in the anything-goes mode. And he *knew* it. When the detective asked him if he'd been with Amber Nickerson on Friday night, he said, 'Who?' Then, 'Maybe,' then, finally, 'Yes.' He knows Amber. He knows her name. He knows he was with her. Amber isn't the only one who regrets Friday night. The defendant regrets it, too. An anything-goes night often leads to a regretful morning. This is just an extreme example."

Pete glances at the outline on his legal pad, then sets it down on counsel table. "I'm not going to go over all the facts again. And I'm not going to spend much time on why Amber did the things she did, why she made the mistakes she made. I talked about that in opening, Mr. Foss talked about it in closing, and you heard from Amber.

"Deciding to report this rape was not an easy step. It took strength. Don't you think it would have been easier for Amber to just *not* report it, to *not* deal with it? Think about how much she's gone through: that night . . . the next day . . . the rape exam . . . the nights since then not sleeping . . . this whole trial. As Mr. Foss said, she would have to be insane to want to go through this if she wasn't actually raped.

"Defense counsel said the sex may have gotten a little rough in this case."

Sundfell moves his chair back.

"But what Mr. Sundfell calls a little rough," Pete continues quickly, "the law calls rape by forcible compulsion."

"Objection."

"Overruled. This is argument."

"Your Honor," Sundfell says, standing, "I want you to—"

"*Overruled.*"

Sundfell sits, slaps his legal pad on the table.

Pete keeps eye contact with the jury during this exchange, hunting for a connection, and one of the women gives him a look he takes as encouraging.

"This case comes down to a simple question," he continues, skipping forward a couple of pages in his mental script. "Do you believe beyond a reasonable doubt that the defendant raped Amber Nickerson? The jury instructions tell you that if you have 'an abiding belief' in the truth of the charge, then you are satisfied beyond a reasonable doubt. The instructions do *not* say you have to know for sure what happened, because almost nothing in life is known for sure. You just need an abiding belief. An abiding belief is, of course, a lasting belief.

"A week from now, a month from now, a year from now, you're going to look back on this trial. You're going to look back, and you're going to want to feel right about your verdict. You're going to look back, and you're going to want to feel that your verdict was just. You're going to look back, and you're going to want to feel that your verdict . . . reflects the truth.

"Please work at this in the jury room, take as much time as you need. You can find the truth, it can be known, you can achieve justice. You can make things right here.

"And you will not only be making things right for the victim, and the community, but for the defendant. Because he knows the truth." Pete maneuvers himself close to Keith, looks right at him. "He knew Amber wasn't consenting, but it was anything goes that night."

Pete then crosses back toward the jury, moving downstage center. "It would be easy to do as defense counsel suggests. Just pretend nobody knows what happened, because then we wouldn't have to deal with it." He stops three feet from the jury box, lowers his voice. "But Amber decided to deal with this. And I trust you will, too.

"The only way to bring real closure to something is to deal with it, to acknowledge the truth, call it the truth, and deal with it as the truth. Only then can everyone put the regret behind.

"Thank you."

Pete is thinking two words as he walks back to counsel table: *scotch* and *water.*

Power, Money, or Art

AS THE jury begins their deliberations, Pete and Scott walk to the J&M Cafe for their first shots of scotch and Jack Daniel's, then catch a bus to Tini Bigs for their third, fourth, and fifth shots, then cab it to the BP, where they buy two forty-ouncers, which they quaff by the Dumpster in the parking lot of Deja Vu.

"Regular or V.I.P?" the bulky doorman in an ill-fitting tuxedo asks.

"Regular," Scott says.

"You can always upgrade to V.I.P," the doorman says.

"We'll keep that in mind."

They make their way toward a table on the far side of the stage. Ubiquitous speakers blast "The Fugue," a dream-pop tune by the Melody Unit that lends a welcome air of unreality to the club.

Though drunk, Pete wonders if he is drunk enough. His eyes adjust as flashing multicolored Fresnels bounce off the wall of mirrors behind the stage. The crowd is sparse, the atmosphere vaguely depressing. A few men sit up around the bar that borders the stage and a few more are in the back on the couches, either receiving lap dances or chatting up the girls.

On stage a reasonably good-looking bleached blonde takes off her top and cups her hands over her breasts, which are much more than a handful.

Almost as soon at Pete and Scott are seated a waitress in black shorts and a white shirt is on them. "What can I get you?"

Pete wonders how many asinine responses she has heard off that poorly phrased question.

"Coke," Scott says.

"Club soda."

"Do you have your tickets?"

As he hands her the tickets, Pete asks, "Do you know if Beth Keller is working tonight?"

"Does she work here?"

"I'm not sure. I heard she used to."

"I'll ask around," she says as she turns away.

Scott looks at Pete. "Beth Keller?"

"Girl I've been having a hard time finding."

"Why don't you just look her up on DISCUS?"

"She's pretty elusive. Stays mobile, apparently."

"Who is she?"

"Long story."

"A stripper from the Bad Old Days?"

Pete shrugs in what could be taken as an affirmative.

"I've always wondered," Scott says, "why do all these strippers have band-guy boyfriends?"

"Some of the girls support guys in bands."

"You've never talked much about those times."

"You've never asked much," Pete says as he pulls out his Camels and lights up. "Which I appreciate."

"Did you imagine you were going to stay with that?" Scott asks. "The rock thing?"

"The plan was to go from 'lonesome to stardom,' which was a line we stole from somewhere. We didn't really have a plan."

"And this is what your life has come to," Scott announces with a sweep of his hand.

"So how's it going with Shannon?"

"She's dropped me. I think."

"You don't know?"

"She's not returning my phone calls."

"Guess you fucked up again."

"Yep. She probably talked to the other waitress I slept with. Who knows? Women, they all talk."

"And men?"

"We do, too, obviously, but we never do it to *discourage* a friend from getting laid. Oh, well, doesn't matter, I would have needed some new soon anyway." Pause. "Next, I'm going for Kim Monroe at 107.7."

"You ever think maybe we should, well, grow up? Or at least I should, since I'm almost ten years older than you."

Scott shakes his head. "No. We've got a criminal justice system that doesn't expect anyone to be a grown-up, we live in a country that doesn't expect anyone to be a grown-up, we've even got a *president* who won't grow up, so why should you?"

"Like the song says, 'To everything there is a season.' "

"I'm not sure what's going on with you, but you've gotta forget this marriage idea. It's a scam—if some guy tries to tell you that marriage and kids and so forth is wonderful, he's lying. He's like Tom Sawyer trying to con someone else into whitewashing the fence with him." Scott pulls out his Lucky Strikes. "People just don't want anyone else to have the fun they're missing."

"Are we having fun?"

"Absolutely." Scott lights up with his Zippo. "In fact, I say we try to hit some new lows tonight."

"We're off to a promising start."

The Melody Unit segues into the Posies, "Any Other Way," a sad song that always picks up Pete's spirits.

"She dropped my hand and said I will go no further . . ."

The dancer, rolling her body to the rhythm, turns around and leans against the mirror with one hand and uses the other to remove her bottoms, which catch on her high heel before she shakes them off.

"Okay," Scott says, "should we talk about the case and then we can put the regret behind us and concentrate on"—he glances back at the dancer—"behinds?"

"I'm going to move to have that remark stricken from the record."

"I had a good time cochairing. I don't know about the verdict, but we won on style points. Might have been the most fun I've had with my clothes on."

"Bob used to always say that if you can't have a normal life—"

"Bob the dead drummer?"

"Yeah. He used to say that if you can't have a normal life, if you can't find love, then you have to religiously devote yourself to one of three things: the pursuit of power, money, or art. He devoted himself to alcohol and drugs, but still."

"Power, money, or art? What about sex?"

"Comes with the other three."

"When you put it that way, it makes sense."

Pete turns his attention in the direction of the dancer, who has taken to doing the splits on stage, her facial expression one Pete associates with activities such as, say, grocery shopping.

The waitress returns with their sodas served in plastic cups with the Sonics logo, which includes a stylized version of the Space Needle. Pete tips her two dollars.

"I asked around," she says, "and one of the girls said Beth moved to Hollywood. But she may not know what she's talking about."

"Okay. Well, thanks."

"Let me know if you need anything else."

Scott checks her out as she steps away. "She'll be dancing here within a month."

"Symbol of the future," Pete says, holding up his cup with the Space Needle logo facing Scott.

"What?"

"Never mind."

"*No, you wouldn't have it any other way . . .*"

The Posies fade out with a rain effect and the dancer exits, picking up her clothes and cash from the side of the stage. Scott claps enthusiastically.

"Let's hear it for Mercedes," the emcee says.

"How about some food at Mama's?" Pete suggests. He dreads sobering up here. "Maybe a few margaritas," he adds as additional incentive for Scott.

"Next up," the emcee says, "Porsche."

"I'm not sure I'm in the mood for Mexican," Scott says as Nirvana's "Heart-Shaped Box" fades in. "And let's at least see what kind of talent is next."

Dark-haired and wearing ripped black stockings, Porsche is surprisingly pretty. She walks nonchalantly out onto the stage, stops, taps her high heels to the beat. "*She eyes me like a Pisces when I am weak . . .*" Pete taps his own foot along.

"Pete?"

Pete turns to see a girl wearing nothing but red panties and a pink T-shirt that is cut short between her breasts and pierced navel: Danielle.

"What are you doing here?" Pete asks.

"I *work* here. What are *you* doing here?"

"I thought you were working at the Lusty."

"Needed more money. I'm only going to be here for another five thousand dollars or so."

"Scott, this is Danielle."

"Felicity. My stage name is Felicity."

"Nice to meet you, Felicity."

"So," she says to Scott, "want a lap dance?"

"A tempting idea," Scott says, and it does not sound like he is just being polite. "But some other time."

"Next song?"

"Pete Tyler! It's you!"

A dancer steps between Pete and the stage, hands on hips, wearing a white bra, large crucifix, and plaid skirt hemmed all the way up to the edge of her white panties. Her dirty blond hair is rubber-banded in pigtails. Pete doesn't recall ever seeing her before.

Scott looks back and forth between them, grinning.

"Do you know him?" Danielle asks her.

"I know who he is," the dancer says. "Beth told me about him."

"Beth?" Pete says.

"Yeah. Wow, you're *here.*"

People are starting to stare.

"You two want to sit?" Pete offers.

Danielle sits next to Scott and helps herself to one of his Lucky Strikes.

The other dancer pulls up a chair beside Pete, close enough that her legs mingle with his. "I'm Lexus."

"You're the third car name I've heard since we arrived," Scott says.

"Actually my real name is Helen."

The waitress appears. "Would you like to buy drinks for the ladies?" she asks.

"No," Scott says.

"Sure," Pete says.

The gals order root beers, which actually sound good to Pete, so he orders one, too.

"Pete Tyler," Helen says when the waitress leaves. "Here you are. I have one of your CDs."

Only CD.

Scott raises his eyebrows. "A fan?"

"A *huge* fan," Helen says. "When I found out that Beth had been your girlfriend, I was like, that's so cool."

"I keep hearing about this girl Beth," Danielle says. "But I've never met her. I'd like to meet her."

"Do you still hang out with her?" Pete asks Helen.

"No, haven't seen her in months."

"Do you know where she is these days?"

"I have no idea. You know how she is."

Pete nods, though he is not sure what she means.

"So, aren't you a lawyer or something now?" Helen asks.

"These two are the prosecutors on the Keith Junior trial," Danielle says.

"No fucking way!"

"Yep," Scott says.

Pete nods.

"Was that your picture in *The Stranger?*" Helen asks. "I didn't read the article."

"Pictures were better than the article," Scott says. "By the way, I like your costume."

"Catholic schoolgirl theme," Helen explains brightly, holding up her small white vinyl purse, which sports a photo of the Pope.

"Where did you get the Pope purse?" Scott asks, as though he is in the market for one.

"Toys in Babeland."

Nirvana's "Heart-Shaped Box" segues into "Alive," from Pearl Jam's first album—"*Son, she said, I've got a little story for you . . .*"

"Please welcome Daydream Believer," the emcee says as a new dancer steps up, pretty, petite, smiling mischievously.

"*Daydream Believer?*" Pete says to Danielle.

"And her real name is Shallan or something like that."

"You know, you're not the only rock star here this evening," Helen says. "What's-his-name from Pearl Jam is also here."

Helen points to a guy on a couch with long dark hair, who is actually what's-his-name from Alice in Chains. Pete sees no purpose in pointing out the subtle distinction.

Daydream Believer also appears to be of the opinion that what's-his-name is from Pearl Jam, because she is mouthing the words to their song and playing it right to him, her tongue stud flashing as she screams along, "*I, I, I'm still alive . . .*"

Then another dancer with pale skin and black hair climbs on stage—and for an unsettling half-beat Pete thinks he's seen Beth. He shakes himself out of it, realizing that whatever Beth looks like now she would not still look seventeen, as this dancer does. Still, he's fixated on her as she flops her arm over the other dancer's shoulder and they play out a mock duet for what's-his-name.

Then another dancer joins the show, and Danielle and Helen

rush up as well, and suddenly the stage fills with nearly a dozen dancers in various stages of nakedness getting into the act.

During the instrumental jams, they divide duties, with one pantomiming drums, three displaying air-guitar skills, and the rest simply tossing off their clothes.

"I, I, I'm still alive . . ."

What's-his-name laughs and headbangs along, while men from the back couches step forward, some clapping, and for the moment everyone is at a rocking great party with excellent music on a big-time sound system and the high they crave just within reach. Though Pete well knows that further down this road lies emptiness and pain and regret, he's in that mood.

The Thing About Kurt Cobain

PETE TWISTS open the oversized cap with the stinging hornet logo and hands the Mickey's Big Mouth to Helen. Then he opens a malt liquor for himself and has a long swig.

Tastes like adolescence.

Beside them are Scott, and Helen's roommate, Hadley—the dancer with the momentary resemblance to Beth. They are sitting back against the bulkhead on the leeward side of the top deck of the ferry steaming across Elliott Bay toward Bainbridge Island. The deck is empty because of the late hour and the breeze. Though it is almost June, the wind off the water swoops up with a biting chill. Smoke from their four cigarettes drifts aft past the yellow deck lights.

Hadley and Helen are both wearing Levi's and Doc Martens, but Helen is wearing a large sweater while Hadley toughs it out with a T-shirt and black leather jacket.

"Are you guys really the ones prosecuting Keith?" Hadley asks.

Pete nods.

"Wow," she says to Pete, "this is *so* . . . I don't know."

Hadley, Pete decides, is the one he would rather sleep with, though the unspoken matchups do not appear to favor that desire.

"Beth made your thing with her sound so romantic," Helen

interjects. "That month in that hotel, listening to music, falling in love, you writing songs."

Drinking so much I threw up.

"And then the way you two kept missing each other the next few years," Helen continues, "like crisscrossed lovers."

Crisscrossed?

"I think she's almost afraid of running into you now," Helen says, "because it might be kind of a letdown."

Pete nods. "Might be."

Beth clearly romanticized and rewrote the story, even more than he did, and Pete likes hearing this, likes the idea of someone once loving him in storybook fashion.

"How do you like working at Deja Vu?" Scott asks Hadley, his voice impressively unslurred.

"It's kind of like being a zoo animal," Hadley says, which sounds like an answer she's given before. "I mean, some of the guys are there and they look at you and they just want to admire what they see and enjoy it. Other guys want to poke sticks at the animals. You know?"

Pete nods. As mystifying as Pete finds women, he did learn to nod understandingly at the stories told to him by the waifs and strays who showed up at his shows and came backstage to find a connection they weren't finding elsewhere, and, at some point after learning to nod, he actually learned to understand a bit.

"Do you still write songs?" Helen asks.

"No."

"You guys were my favorite band," she says, "until Nirvana came along. But then they became too fucking popular. In some ways it's kind of cool that you broke up after the one record. It's like you guys will always be cool." Helen tosses her cigarette, which twirls in a sparkling arc over the side. "What's Todd doing now?"

"He's married, producing records in L.A."

"I read that it was his idea to quit."

"Quit after he met Ruth," Pete says. "Said he only wanted to

be in a band so that someone would love him, and once someone did, he didn't feel motivated anymore."

"He said that?"

"Well, not exactly, but that was the gist of it."

"That's kind of romantic," Hadley says.

"You think you guys might ever get back together?" Helen
asks. "You and Todd and some other drummer?"

"No."

Pete looks over at Hadley as she takes a long drink of the
Mickey's, and he wonders how he is going to swing the switch.
He doubts Scott will care one way or the other, even if he is
sober enough to notice.

"Did you know Kurt Cobain?" Helen asks.

Pete looks back at her, nods.

"*Really?*" Helen says. "Did you hang out with him?"

"No, we just played a couple of the same shows."

Pete has some good Cobain stories, but does not like telling
them. He stares out at the lights of West Seattle as they pass Alki
Point. The wind picks up and he cups his cigarette.

"Did you know Courtney?" Helen asks.

Had drunken sex once. "No."

"The thing about Kurt Cobain," Helen says, "is that he never
wanted to be a star. It just happened. Who would have thought
from *Bleach* and their other Sub Pop stuff that they could be the
next big thing?"

"David Geffen," Scott offers.

"Okay, maybe, but the thing about Kurt is he never lost his
artistic integrity. He always gave off this incredible thing of
pureness."

"He was just a fucked-up guy with a lot of talent," Hadley
says.

Pete is surprised by this and wonders if Hadley met Cobain
somewhere along the local club trail.

"But the thing about Kurt," Helen continues, "is—"

"The thing about Kurt Cobain," Pete says, "is that he's dead."

This proves to be a conversation killer.

Pete leans his head back and looks at the almost full moon as it's exposed by a break in the clouds. He tosses his empty Mickey's in the general direction and it falls out of sight. Hadley does the same a beat later.

Scott, meanwhile, tries to salvage the situation by pulling more Mickey's out of the brown grocery bag and passing them around.

"No, thanks," Pete says.

Scott looks confused.

"I don't want to be trapped on Bainbridge until the next ferry run tomorrow." Pete surprises himself with this foresight. "I'm going back on the return trip."

"Don't you want to see Hadley and Helen's abode?" Scott says. "It's a *double-wide mobile*."

"I'm glad I had a chance to meet you," Pete says to Helen and Hadley. "But I've got to get back to Seattle." To Scott he says, "Sorry."

"Well," Scott says, "I guess this just means more Mickey's for the three of us."

"You don't seem like your songs," Helen suddenly says to Pete.

"What?"

"It's like you're not even that guy anymore."

Hell's Like Teen Spirit

PETE BUYS a bottle of Talking Rain water and drinks it on the car deck near the open bow, the brisk wind and salt spray sobering him up.

The Seattle skyline shines on the slope above Elliott Bay, the downtown lights zigzagging across the rippled water. The Smith Tower with its brightly lit steeple, Seattle's tallest building in Pete's mother's day, seems stubby next to the Columbia Tower. Pete wonders how this image will change in the next millennium, if he will be around to see the changes. He's already lived to be older than he thought possible in his twenties.

After disembarking, Pete walks south on Alaskan Way, cuts east on Columbia. Light rain begins falling and so he picks up the pace, jogging as well as he can in his wingtips. A Gray Top cab pulls out in front of him on Second Avenue and he flags it down.

Entering the back, he is not surprised to hear Nirvana's "Smells Like Teen Spirit" on the radio, the live version, which he prefers. Wet, and short of breath, he gives the cabbie directions while Cobain screams—"*our little tribe has always been and . . .*"

Two dollars plus tip later, Pete steps out on Jackson Street. He walks down the alley, eyeing the fire escape. The ladder, however, is about ten feet off the ground.

Pete makes a standing jump that is at least a foot short. Then he steps back a few feet, remembers how he used to be able to dunk a basketball—forgetting this was about fifteen years ago—and tries to put himself in that mind. He loosens up a little, then takes four quick steps and leaps. His outstretched fingers fly toward the step, but several inches short.

Pete's wingtips slide out from under him when he lands and his palms instinctively snap out and cushion his butt's impact on the wet pavement. He sits for a moment, then stands slowly when he feels the wetness soak through his pants.

From this vantage point he realizes there is a Dumpster only twenty feet away. Using the ingenuity that occasionally separates us from the rest of the animal kingdom, Pete wheels the Dumpster under the fire escape ladder, his hands pushing near the DO NOT PLAY ON OR AROUND sticker.

He then easily grabs the ladder and, watching his footing, climbs the fire escape.

A light comes on above.

"Pete?" Esmé's head pokes out her window.

"Hi."

"What the hell is all the noise?"

"Me."

"Did you try the phone?"

"I was afraid you wouldn't let me in."

"Well, you got that right."

He continues up to her window. "This was harder than it looks."

Esmé is wearing nothing but a T-shirt, as far as Pete can tell, and though she is not likely wearing lipstick, her lips are promisingly red.

"You look good," he says.

"You," she says, "look like hell."

"Can I come in?"

"No."

"No?"

"No."

Pete had not anticipated this contingency, and he does not

know quite how to deal with it. "Come on," he says. Begging becomes his fall-back plan.

"What would you think if I just let you in right now?"

"I'd think you were a kind-hearted soul," he tries, "who wants to ease the world's suffering in whatever small way she can."

"Pete, I was falling for you."

He runs a hand through his wet hair, sweeping it off his forehead. "And you must have been able to tell how I felt about you."

"No," she says, "I couldn't. But that's not the point. The point is I let myself fall for you and we decided to break it off and I don't want to stretch out the pain. I'm moving back home, and then I'm going to law school." Her eyes are wet. "I'm not looking for an FTF thing. And I can't believe you show up at three A.M. like this looking to fuck."

"Esmé, no. That's not why I'm here." *Not totally.*

She looks at him for a long beat, her mouth slightly open, her wet eyes unblinking. Pete has to stop himself from staring at her nipples.

"The police are probably going to show up pretty soon," she finally says.

"That's okay. I'll probably know them."

"Pete . . ."

"Could I come in, please?"

"I can't keep doing this to myself. I can't keep falling for the wrong guys, making the same dumb mistakes."

"What do you mean?"

"I'd rather be alone," she says, "than keep doing this to myself."

"Nobody really wants to be alone."

"There are worse things."

"What? What's worse?"

"Good night," she says, and closes the window. A moment later the venetian blinds drop in a fast clatter.

Ted Bundy Was a
Local Law Student

AFTER TWO days of deliberation the jury presents a written question to the judicial assistant.

Pete, Scott, Sundfell, Satan's Little Helper, and the defendant are called into court. Judge Sorensen emerges from chambers without his robe, wearing paint-stained jeans and a work shirt, holding a piece of paper from a yellow legal pad.

"I just wanted to put this on the record," he says to the attorneys, and the court reporter begins typing. "The jury has asked a question. The question is, 'How long do we have to argue about Rape 2 before we can move to the lesser offense of Rape 3?'"

Sundfell smiles.

"Any suggestions?" the judge asks.

"Until someone is seriously injured," Scott says.

"We defer to the court, Your Honor," Pete says.

"I'm going to answer, 'Until there is no reasonable likelihood of a unanimous verdict.' Any objections?"

"No, sir," Pete says.

"Well . . ." Sundfell starts to say, but Sorensen scowls at him. "No, Your Honor."

The judge writes this out on the paper and hands it to Trish. "I'm going to go home and work on my garage," he announces. "There's a leak in the roof."

Sundfell whispers something to Sue, who escorts the defendant out of the courtroom. Sundfell then turns to Pete and Scott. "You guys want to talk?"

"No," Scott says.

"About an offer," Sundfell says.

"We made an offer earlier," Pete says. "You want to make a counteroffer?"

Sundfell checks to make sure Keith Junior is gone, then says, "They're hanging on Rape 2, and whoever is hanging them on Rape 2 is probably going to hang them on Rape 3. If they believe her, they should find him guilty of Rape 2. There's no reason to hang on Rape 2 and convict on Rape 3."

"That's true," Pete says, "logically. But this is a jury."

"You gave an outstanding rebuttal argument," Sundfell says to Pete, then turns to Scott. "And you did a hell of a job, too."

"Good enough for government work," Scott says.

"What's up, Sundfell? Why are you acting civil?"

"He'll take an Assault 3 right now. Low end. No sexual motivation."

Pete shakes his head.

"Or an Assault 4 with sexual motivation. Then you can stick him with a year of counseling and drug treatment, which he probably needs anyway."

"I told you what would happen before you would get a misdemeanor out of us," Scott says.

"Assault 3, sexual motivation," Pete says.

Sundfell shakes his head. "I can't plead him to something where he would have to register. Come on, guys. He's not a perv, he's not a Ted Bundy. He's just a hard-drinking, hard-smoking, drug-abusing, compulsive, fucked-up musician. Pete, this is just a guy who's got to get his life under control, not someone who needs to go to jail and then register as a sex offender. Think about it. I know almost everyone in the prosecutor's office dislikes me—"

"Don't sell yourself short," Scott says. "Almost everyone who works in this courthouse dislikes you."

"Okay, but try to put that aside. Please."

After Sundfell clears out, Scott turns to Pete.

" 'Please'? What the fuck was *that* about? He should be rubbing our noses in this, and instead he's begging?"

"I heard a rumor that his client wanted to plead."

"So why didn't he?"

"Sundfell?"

Sub Pop, Fizz Fizz

"THIS COULD be a kick," Katie says as they climb into the Pioneer taxi outside Pete's loft. She wears a black dress and pearls. "Who's going to be at this hootenanny?"

"It's Sub Pop, so, you know."

"The old tribe of crazies, junkies, sluts, crybabies and ne'er-do-wells."

"Yep."

"And Beth?"

"I doubt it. And it doesn't matter, because a stripper told me I'm 'not that guy anymore.' "

"What?"

"Never mind."

"Are you going to be shunned because of the Keith Junior case?"

" 'Shunned.' Perfect word, but I'm just looking for this one gal who works there."

"Who?"

"You don't know her."

"Is she part of your quest for a bride? How's that going?"

He lowers a window. "I'm hoping the darkest hour is just before the dawn." He lights a cigarette.

"Still trying to quit?"

"Yeah. How's mother doing?"

"She took Sandy to the vet today."

"Why?"

"She's getting old—her hips are hurting. The vet gave her some painkillers that seem to help."

"So now even the family dog is going to have a drug problem."

Katie laughs. "What's up with you and Winter?"

"I don't know."

"You're not serious about her, are you?"

"I don't know," he says. "There's something about her I love. She's been through a lot and survived it well."

"I mean you're not serious about her as someone to marry."

"Maybe."

"Be careful, Pete. Both people bring a lot of past baggage to a marriage, and that's fine—as long as you're aware of it."

"I know, little sis." He flicks his ash out the window. "Does Mom ever talk to you about missing the old drunk?"

"Yes, she does. You know, I didn't realize he was a drunk until I was in my twenties."

"Neither did I," Pete says. "Everyone in the Washington State Patrol apparently did, but I guess he gets some credit for keeping it from us."

"He was a good father."

"That's debatable."

"He was."

"I didn't mean I really wanted to debate it."

"Gotta let the past go, Pete."

Pete nods after a beat. He used to hate losing arguments to his sister, but now just accepts it.

At the Showbox entrance Pete hands over his invite, ushers in Katie as his "plus one." He suspects it was a typical oversight that his name was not deleted from the Sub Pop mailing list.

Just beyond the coat check a large black-and-white banner with the Sub Pop logo reads:

GOING OUT OF BUSINESS FOR ELEVEN YEARS

"*Cat!*" Kim Warnick runs across the room toward Katie and then stops a foot in front of her, arms held open, Budweiser in hand. Katie hugs her. "Where the hell have you been?" Kim asks.

"Having a life."

"Wow," Kim says. "I wonder what *that's* like." She turns to Pete and hugs him. "Hello, Counselor."

"Good to see you," Pete says. "Thanks for coming to watch the closing argument, and thanks for sitting on the right side."

"Hey, I *love* watching your trials. Have you been reading the coverage in *The Stranger?*"

Pete shakes his head.

"They've been making fun of you. They printed the lyrics of that old song of yours, 'Felony Girl.' I thought it was almost clever of them."

Kurt Bloch sidles over and says hello, acts as though it has not been years since he saw Katie, then takes Kim away by the arm, quizzing her about sound problems.

Hype, a documentary about the Seattle music scene, silently shows Tacoma's Seaweed from "Grungefest '93" on a wall. Below the projection are dozens of faded flyers from old shows: the Mentors at the Bird, Mudhoney and Tad and Nirvana at the Moore Theater, Moving Parts and the Untouchables at the Gorilla Room, Girl Trouble and the Thrown-Ups at the Central, the Ramones and the Meyce at, oddly, the Olympic Hotel Georgian, the Fastbacks, Skin Yard, and his own band Morph at Ditto, the Melvins and Nirvana and the Dwarves at the Motor Sports Int'l Garage, with the Melvins headlining.

"I'm going to go get a beer," Katie says.

Pete continues to scan the flyers until he is snapped out of his nostalgic reverie by Al Bloch, Kurt's brother.

"Hey."

They shake hands. Pete has not seen Al in several years and Al looks good but older, and it occurs to Pete that he, too, must look older. This thought should not startle Pete, but does.

"You still living in L.A.?" Pete asks.

"Yeah, Silverlake. Just flew up for this."

"You see Simonds around in L.A.?"

"He's producing some movie with Adam Sandler. Doing his part to infantilize the culture."

"How about Moritz?"

"Surfin', stonin', and bonin', I don't know."

"And Joanou?"

"Did a video for some friends of mine."

"How about you? What have you been up to?"

"Well, I got married."

"No shit?"

"Six months ago. Thinking about having a kid."

"How is it? Marriage?"

"Good. It was time, you know."

Pete nods. "I'm getting married, too. I haven't figured out to whom yet, though."

Al laughs, apparently assuming this is a joke.

"This is a long shot," Pete says, "but do you remember Beth Keller?"

"Of course. I had kind of a thing for her." Al notices Pete's reaction. "You went out with her for a while, didn't you?"

"Sort of. Do you know what happened to her?"

Al shakes his head. "I don't know. I don't know what happens to all those people."

Pete nods. "Want to get a beer?"

"I've gotta go help Kurt with something, but I'll catch up with you later."

Pete walks alone through the lounge area looking for Esmé. He receives a few sideways glances and some outright stares and starts to feel like the uncool kid at a high school party—one of his worst fears.

Jonathan Poneman, Sub Pop's "Executive Chairman of Supervisory Management," who is wearing bunny ears for no reason Pete can imagine, either ignores Pete or does not see him. Poneman is talking to Carol, the artist, who is with a guy Pete presumes to be her guitarist boyfriend, and KISW deejay Scott Vanderpool.

Zera, a stunning blonde dressed like an Aztec sacrifice, acknowledges Pete with a wave, but she is also with her boyfriend, a guy in a band that relocated here like so many fungible others, another incumbent who puts Pete in mind of the Joe Jackson song.

A girl Pete does not even know scowls at him. Susie Tennant and Meg Watjen say hello—*God bless them!*—as he passes the table where they're sitting with Jack Endino and a lesbian socialist named Trudy Castro who is rumored to be a sure bet in the upcoming city council election.

The two tallest guys at the party are, as usual, Krist Novoselic and a writer from L.A. named Bick something, part of the still growing Southern Cal contingent. They're talking with deejay Bill Reid, another tall guy.

Esmé is nowhere in sight.

The first two drinks of the night are free with admission tickets, which explains the crowd at the bar. Pete orders a beer and a scotch.

While he's waiting, Rose, a.k.a. Vomit Girl, appears. "Hi," she says to Pete.

"Hi, how are you?"

"Shitty," she says. "Greg Dulli just snubbed me. Who is he to snub me? He's not even *from* Seattle. The *loser.*"

Pete takes his scotch and beer and says goodbye to Rose. He hopes he is not so desperate that he will be looking for Rose in an hour, but does not rule it out.

Everett True, the rarely sober, often confrontational music critic from *The Stranger,* is perched in a mock carnival booth by the far wall. Traci Vogel, Brad Steinbacher, and Kathleen Wilson, also from *The Stranger,* all look scared by whatever Mr. True is saying. Pete steers clear of this on his way backstage.

He spots Eddie Vedder in the hallway with his wife, Beth, from the band Hovercraft. She's pretty, dark-haired, cool-looking.

Vedder perplexes Pete because he is, according to local folklore, monogamous. Any beautiful woman in the world would have sex with him: models, actresses, heiresses, porn stars, and, of course, the thousands of young girls who come to Pearl Jam shows and lose it during "Daughter." Hell, Pete figures, most *guys* would sleep with Vedder—*the man wrote the lyrics to "Black."*

Pete wants to yell at Vedder, "*How?* How do you *not* have sex with all these beautiful women who can make a man momentarily immortal?"

"Pete?"

He turns.

Resa, a girlfriend of Kim's who looks like a supermodel shrunken to five-foot-four, grabs him. "They're about to go on."

Pete follows her behind the curtains, past the absent security, just as the band is directed toward the stage by a roadie with a flashlight.

Resa points to stage left. Pete steps on top of one of the equipment boxes stacked against the wall, positioning himself to have a view. Resa hops up with him.

Pete scans the crowd, does not see Esmé.

The Fastbacks take the stage unceremoniously. Lulu crosses to stage left, holding a Gibson that appears to outweigh her, looking exactly how she has looked for as long as Pete can remember. Kim takes center stage with the white Fender bass Duff McKagan gave her. Mike steps up to the drums. Kurt crosses to stage right where he receives the traditional tossing of plastic cups, which are, for the moment, empty. He picks up his red 1961 Epiphone Wilshire and starts tuning, but no sound comes out. Scott McCaughey quickly appears to check connections, wearing sunglasses.

The crowd starts to grow and move forward as they realize the show is about to begin. Some young guys from a band with the unfortunate moniker Urine Tubes make their way to front and center, right beside some members of Keith Junior's old band. This is not a good mix. Old school versus new school, and some of the new boys are close friends with Amber.

Kim seems to notice this development at about the same time Pete does. She steps to the edge of the stage as the male musicians mouth off to each other. Pete cannot hear the voices from this distance, but he recognizes the testosterone posturing. Kim says something to them, but not into the microphone, so Pete cannot hear this either.

Harvey Danger singer Sean Nelson then steps between the two factions, apparently playing peacemaker. Gabe, the all-purpose roadie for the Murder City Devils, appears on the scene and taps Sean on the shoulder. Sean turns, says something. Gabe punches Sean in the mouth. Sean crumples.

This serves as a starting flag for the Urine Tubes and Keith's friends, who instantly go all out at each other, swinging and kicking and grabbing.

"Hey, we need cleanup on aisle six," Kim yells into her microphone. "Someone spilled blood."

At first the crowd retreats and forms a semicircle for the guys to duke it out, but the line between participants and spectators collapses as friends rush in to help friends or deck enemies, and in seconds the fracas spreads and fights break out all over the floor like it's a hockey game played in flannel and black leather. Half a dozen bouncers rush out from backstage, but they only add to the chaos.

Kim, Lulu, and Mike step offstage. Kurt and McCaughey continue trying to get sound from Kurt's guitar amp.

Pete lights a Camel, enjoys the skirmish.

"Boys are so dumb," Resa says. "I'm going backstage."

"See ya."

Suddenly there's a buzz and a screech as Kurt's amp comes to life. He begins playing the chords for "New Book of Old," loosely improvising, almost as though he's synching up with the action on the floor, and it puts Pete in mind of the piano men who used to play live soundtracks for silent movies.

As the fisticuffs degenerate into wrestling, and people start splashing beer onto the diehards, Pete heads for the exit, edging his way around the periphery.

"This is for Keith," someone says, and the significance does not register with Pete.

Then suddenly he is blindsided by a punch to the side of his face—his cigarette flies out of his mouth and he nearly falls, but he knows it would be suicide to hit the floor here, so he struggles to stay on his feet as he backs up. When the guy keeps coming at him he swings low for his crotch and connects and the guy actually goes "*Oooofff.*"

Straight On Till Morning

DRIZZLE FALLS lightly on Pete's face and the night air tastes good and seems to help. He touches his right eye, notes the dab of blood on his finger. Many of the guests are taking the opportunity to leave and there are not enough taxis to cover the exodus.

Katie arrives at Pete's side. "What the hell?"

"Huh?"

"Why were *you* in that half-witted brawl?"

"I wasn't, but someone took a poke at me anyway."

Pete pulls out his pack of Camels, flips one into his mouth. He leans over, shelters the cigarette with his shoulders, lights up.

"I'm glad we went out like this," Katie says. "It'll remind me for the next few years why I don't go out anymore."

"Why don't you tell me and then I'll know, too."

She pulls an impossibly small cell phone out of her purse, along with a tissue she hands to Pete.

"Who are you calling?" he asks. "Taxi?"

"William." She punches in a number.

"In Bellevue?"

"No, he's out with the boys tonight in the big city."

"So you're going to cut short his fun?"

"And you know what?" she says, bringing the phone to her

face. "He's going to be *happy* to hear from me and then take me home to bed. What are *you* going to do?"

Pete looks up at a break in the wind-blown clouds and can see a few dimly visible stars. When he and Katie were kids, she would say, "Which way to Never-never Land?" and he would answer, "First star on the left, straight on till morning."

Another One in the Top Ten

PETE REFUSES to be taken home, so William and Katie drop him off at the Fenix Underground on Jackson and Second. As he bails out of the Ardennes-green Range Rover he notices the two of them exchange a look, something from the world of subtle adult-couple gestures he cannot quite decipher, and it enhances the melancholy creeping up on him.

The Retros are opening for the Beatniks, and Pete walks in on a workmanlike cover of "Tainted Love," which the audience sings along with. "*Sometimes I feel I've got to*"—clap, clap—"*run away . . .*"

At the bar Pete orders a shot of scotch from an attractive gal with an eyebrow ring and it is a generous shot and so he orders another. She does not linger to flirt, which disappoints him.

"Tainted Love" fades down and out and, contrary to Pete's expectation, the band does *not* segue into "Where Did Our Love Go." He is outraged. How can a band cover "Tainted Love" and not follow up with "Where Did Our Love Go" per the definitive dance mix? He shakes his head in dismay as he exits.

He has walked about two blocks before he realizes he is heading toward Esmé's. Down the alley there's the Dumpster, still under the fire escape. Pete hoists himself up, climbs onto the fire escape, and proceeds up to Esmé's window.

The blinds are not drawn. In fact, Pete realizes upon closer examination, there are no blinds. The wind blows the rain in streaks down the window and he wipes a section clear with his forearm.

He sticks his face to the window, cups his hands around his eyes, and sees emptiness: no furniture, hardwood in need of sweeping, the refrigerator pulled back from the wall, door wide open, no interior light.

Pete can already feel this image burning its way into his Top Ten Regrets.

Carnival Desires

PETE WALKS home under the Alaskan Viaduct to avoid the rain. The two A.M. traffic above sounds like a rushing river. If he were in a movie—and the more things go wrong, the more he thinks this way—the soundtrack might fade in with something like "The Killing Moon" by Echo and the Bunnymen, or R.E.M.'s "Losing My Religion," or maybe the Smashing Pumpkins cover of Fleetwood Mac's "Landslide," and the thought of this depresses the holy hell out of him.

There have been many times in Pete's younger years when he thought himself ennobled by loneliness, but now he cannot summon up this trick.

He just feels like a fuck-up.

His mind wanders to his various girlfriends and semi-girlfriends, and he decides to order them chronologically, with the half-baked idea that an insight lurks in the list: *Judy, fifth grade, wrote notes signed S.W.A.K. Terry, eighth grade, pink lipstick, first kiss, heard she died in a car accident. In the summer after ninth grade there was the girl on Jones Island who wore vanilla-coconut suntan lotion, name forgotten. Then in high school there was Kit, skipped school to have sex, no idea what you were doing. Lorraine, cheerleader, sex in the bathroom at Kay's party, a high school high point. Liz, double dated with Chris and Darcy, inspiration for some godawful poetry. Mary, goth, sexy, shy, Bowie fan, ignored her at school because she was not part of cool clique and you're still ashamed of this. Kerin, astounding body, wonderful mouth, cool attitude, first oral sex, always thought of her when band did punk version of "Wouldn't It Be Nice." In college there was Sarah, smart, beautiful, mildly dysfunctional, Beatles lover, near perfect. Michelle, obsessed with Marilyn Monroe, modeled, traveled, exchanged letters and compilation cassettes. Mary, tall and beautiful but something missing. Jayne the Canadian, witty, confused, spent many nights in the convertible, prone to crying jags after sex. Rachel, perfect skin, turned you onto Anaïs Nin, seemed crazy as a loon, but probably wasn't. Jill, sorority girl but cool, marriage material but no way, you didn't know what to do with that. Then there were the prodigious days in the band with mostly one- and two-nighters, but the occasional something more. Beth, first love. Sara, actress, small perfect breasts, fun with Coronas, best remembered for those nights that started with Bob and Pilar. Rene, model, astounding cheekbones, eventually married Slash of Guns N' Roses, but "we'll always have the Grand Canyon." Sydney who quit drinking after Valentine's bender together, continually said she was "too smart to be an actress," might have been right. Holly, witty, oral, mischievous, can still picture her in the swimming pool. Alexis, lithe model, cool but goofy, turned you on to Leonard Cohen, does TV commercials now. Marina, classically pretty, highly presentable, issues, but maybe should have proposed to her anyway, a Drink & Dial favorite until her marriage, which stung a little. Ashley, sharp sense of humor, saved you on some dark nights, but would not have intercourse without promise of monogamy so did not happen. Dylan, fair-skinned and pretty, actually seemed to understand poetry, preferred drugs. Molly, L.A. girl, good mouth, lively eyes, various hair colors, mad about band not staying in L.A., best remembered for singing Kate Pierson's part when band covered Iggy Pop's "Candy." Chloe, most attractive waitress ever at the Olive, more than a one-night stand but not sure what more, turned you on to Jane's Addiction. Denise, cool, sarcastic, said her mouth was too small for blow jobs, not true. Tracy, witty, good heart, good mouth, world-class massages. Michelle redux. Then in law school there was Lisa, smart and pretty, wrote hilarious notes and song parodies, liked both hard core and Pearl Jam. Stu, fun, young, stylish, liked trashy novels and trashy movies, modeling in New York now. Tina, great body, great stories, beautiful face but sad eyes, stripper who knew when to quit, Elvis Costello fan. Mollyanne, friend of Tina's, Nirvana fan, Valium prescription, "thin, toned, and stoned," now dancing in Las Vegas? And as a prosecutor there was Hollie, uncomfortable with her good looks, skittish, left town to work in Silicon Valley, nervous breakdown by thirty? April, singer, great legs, great voice, still listen for her music left of the dial. Nariko, art student, into Dead Can Dance, suddenly returned to Japan. Faith, charming, worldly, but limited time because of daughter. Penny, quiet beauty, moved to Seattle from Juneau, Alaska, didn't like "Northern Exposure," liked the Red Hot Chili Peppers. And then Winter and Esmé. And Marie and Heather, a.k.a. Princess & Slave, the only three-way since band broke up and so deserving of honorable mention.*

Lightheaded with recollections, Pete pictures Clarence the Angel turning to Jimmy Stewart in the cemetery and saying, "*See, you really have had a wonderful life.*"

Pete's most interesting experiences, his most intense experiences, his few transcendent experiences, have almost all involved women or music—*music & women = truth & beauty*—and he feels justified in pursuing women with senseless passion because he does not know what life ought to be if not the pursuit of experiences and connections that elevate us, at least for a few moments.

He has absentmindedly wandered past his building and up to Victor Steinbrueck Park, a concrete patio looking out on Elliott Bay primarily frequented by homeless alcoholics. Pete sits on the only vacant bench and lights a Camel. A dirty, dimly lit place where he can mutter to himself.

He wonders if there is a pattern to his romantic mishaps. If he were a Mozart of romance, would he see the patterns and repetitions? If he listened closely, would the tune come to him at last—"*when all is one and one is all, to be a rock and not to roll.*" He laughs. Late-night giddiness has kicked in and no one around him minds.

Thinking of all his ex-girlfriends and the women he had sex with who were not quite girlfriends, and then even the ones he had sex with who were essentially strangers, all the wildly different types of bodies and looks—each one hauntingly beautiful to him in some way—and the only pattern he can see at the moment is, well, *you'll sleep with just about anyone.*

A Horse with No Name

PETE TOSSES his suit jacket over a kitchen stool. One advantage of bachelorhood is that he can leave wet clothes wherever. The disadvantage is that he has ruined expensive suits this way.

Knowing he will not be able to sleep despite the lateness of hour, he wrestles off his wingtips and climbs into the hammock with *The Sportswriter*.

After reading about ten pages with no comprehension, he simply skips to the last two pages. Maybe he can fool his body into thinking he just read a full book, and thereby earn some shuteye.

When Pete first read this book, more than ten years ago, he understood well the moments of recurring boyish joy, the "new living" Mr. Ford writes of, but in his wide-eyed stage he did not realize there would come a time when he would *not* feel those moments for long stretches of time, when he would need to rely on memories to remind himself of possibilities. Somehow the possibilities are starting to swim away from him of late.

Assorted lost options spin in his mind, things he had wanted to do and has not done and will never do. He will never be young and living in New York City, he will never know if he could have been a college athlete and maybe even a pro, he will never sleep with the girl with perfect ankles outside Sean and

Jon's Bar, or the girl with the red umbrella running for the bus, and so it goes.

Pete has tried to go down all the roads he could and yet feels he has missed too many. He has spent his life trying to keep his options open, but he is coming to recognize that this cannot be done indefinitely, and, worse, there is a cost to trying.

Suddenly Pete fears he is lost in a desert. He actually pictures himself walking on cracked baked clay, surrounded by cacti, and he comes to a deep foaming river—*in a desert?*—and there are green fields on the other side but he cannot get across because he has lost his horse and there is no bridge and he cannot swim with all his clothes on.

Then he passes out in the hammock.

Several Dim Bulbs

JUDGE SORENSEN allows television cameras in for the verdict and the courtroom is buzzing with media and with most of the people who were there for opening statement, but also Detective Tuiaia, Winter, Amber, and a few of her friends, and Danielle, who has her blond hair up in a schoolmarmish bun.

When Pete, Scott, Sundfell, Keith, and Sue—who is wearing a leather miniskirt for the occasion—are all in place, Judge Sorensen enters.

"Bring out the jury," he instructs.

The jurors file in, visibly struck by the crowd and the cameras.

"Please be seated," the judge says.

There is a loud rustle followed by a tense silence.

"Would the foreman please stand?" the judge says.

The jury instructions refer to this person as the 'presiding juror,' but Judge Sorensen is not up with the times.

A fiftyish man stands. This is one of the jurors Pete did not have a feel for.

"I understand you have reached a verdict," the judge says.

"No, Your Honor."

"*No?*" The judge turns to Trish.

"I told her we had a *decision*," the presiding juror explains.

"We call that a verdict around here."

"But we don't have a verdict. We couldn't reach a verdict."

Judge Sorensen is exasperated. "What exactly do you mean?"

"We reached a decision that we couldn't reach a verdict."

"On either count?"

"On either count."

Judge Sorensen switches into his judicial voice. "Is there any likelihood of a unanimous verdict in a reasonable amount of time?"

"No, no chance. We're starting to really get on each other's nerves—it's getting stressful."

"Well, I'm sure all the parties are sorry that this trial has caused you stress," Judge Sorensen says with undisguised sarcasm, "but now we're going to have to go through the whole thing again with a new group of jurors. And I don't know what the problem is, but—"

Trish turns to the judge and lightly slaps her face as though she is just remembering something, a signal she often uses that translates as: *shut up before you say something you'll regret.* "I'll take them back to the jury room now," she says, already on the move.

His Honor sighs, then addresses the attorneys. "I'm keeping the case. We'll take a few days off, then start picking a new jury Monday. I hope they're more decisive than the bunch we just had." He steps off the bench.

Pete turns and Amber is sitting in the first row behind him. She looks devastated. Pete steps toward the rail separating them, and is about to say something, when suddenly the defendant appears in front of her.

"Amber," he says, "I am so fucking sorry about this."

Sundfell rushes over, "Keith, don't say anything," but Keith knocks away Sundfell's arm.

"I am so fucking sorry," Keith repeats. "I honestly didn't realize what the hell I did, until . . . well, until I had to sit through this whole stupid fucking thing. I'm sorry for putting you through all this shit."

Keith Junior then walks away, flipping off the cameras.

"The finger is a nice touch of class," Scott says.

Sundfell locks eyes with Pete because they both know something that Keith Junior apparently does not know or did not care about: Pete can hang him with this admission in the retrial. Several witnesses heard it, including Detective Tuiaia, and it may even be on camera.

Pete shifts his eyes to Amber, who is crying as Danielle holds her. He is always fascinated by these courtroom displays of unabashed emotion, but he turns away, sits. He writes on his yellow legal pad, then slides it over to Scott. *Time to make another offer?*

Scott says, "I don't know if we should make a critical decision like this sober."

If Sheep Had Wings

PETE AND Scott kick back in a booth at the Crocodile.

"We've got the son of a bitch cold," Scott says. "He's lying in a coffin, passed out, the sun is coming over the hill and I've got the stake held to his heart and all you've got to do is swing the hammer." He drains his fourth Jack and Coke. "We're like Caesar. Thumbs down, his life is over, thumbs up, he lives."

Pete admires the effortless segue from gothic to gladiator imagery.

"Ahhh, the rush of capricious power," Scott adds, reaching for his Lucky Strikes. "What to do? Mercy or no?"

Pete lights a Camel and leans his head back and watches the smoke rise and fade. One of the winged sheep hanging from the ceiling comes slowly into his focus.

"What's up with the sheep?" Pete says.

Scott looks. "What do you mean?"

"What's up with the wings?"

" 'If sheep had wings they could fly.' "

"No. It's 'If *pigs* had wings they could fly.' "

Scott shrugs. "I don't know. It's art."

Elvis Has Left the Building

PETE IS home and does not want to be alone. The Drink & Dial mood comes over him, but he does not know who to call. He turns on 107.7 and Brian and Marco are riffing on Jason Finn's failure to give up cigarettes, which reminds Pete of his own losing battle, and why he does not like to risk the radio.

He decides he needs a Resurrection Jukebox. Standing in front of his CDs, he considers possible themes, but nothing seems like it will move him.

First sign of the long fade to death?

He climbs into the hammock, and for the second night in a row he falls asleep without going to bed.

The phone rings, startling him. As the answering machine clicks on he looks at the wall clock: just a few minutes past three A.M.

"Peter," his mother says, "are you awake?"

He stumbles out of the hammock and picks up the cordless. "Is something wrong?"

"I thought I heard something downstairs, and so I called Sandy. You know how she always sleeps outside my door, but she wasn't there."

"Mother, I'm sure she's—"

"She's dead. I found her in the backyard. She went out to the garden and died."

The Son Also Rises

PETE DIGS Sandy's grave in the garden on the southeast side of the house, between the zucchini and the Walla Walla onions. The location is his mother's choice, the time choice—pushing four A.M.—his. He did not want to deal with a corpse stiffened by rigor mortis.

The earth is soft for the first couple feet and the digging goes quickly and easily, but then he encounters sand and hard clay. When his fingers feel like they are blistering, he decides he is deep enough.

Sandy is lying just a few feet away, curled up the way she would for sleep. Pete works his hands under her body and lifts. Her legs straighten. He carries her to the grave and lowers her slowly.

This accomplished, Pete crosses himself, remembers a nun telling him that animals don't have souls, which he did not believe then and does not believe now. Then he begins shoveling the dirt back into the hole.

Done, he lights a cigarette. The smoke rises straight up into the cold windless air. He stares at the lake, which is glassy calm all the way to the bridge.

His mother appears from around the corner of the house, wearing an oversized Nordic sweater and carrying two cups of coffee.

Pete takes the larger mug. "Thanks."

"What happened to your eye?"

"Long story."

"And I thought you quit smoking."

"Well, I lied."

"Apparently."

"Still trying." He drops the unfiltered butt next to the zucchini and grinds it into the earth.

"Peter," she says, "I don't mean to be critical."

He shrugs. "I know."

"I'm proud of you. We were both proud of you."

"Thanks, but what the hell are you talking about?"

"I feel like you hide things from me because you think I'm too critical."

"No, I just hide things because . . . otherwise my life would horrify you."

"You'd be surprised what I can handle."

"Want to hear what I did for my twenty-seventh birthday?"

"I don't need to know everything. I just want you to be happy. I want you to know that as you get older, you're going to find things that will give you a deeper, sweeter, more lasting satisfaction than whatever it is you've been chasing since you entered puberty and became crazy. Trust me on this."

Pete nods. *Want too much, end up with nothing.*

"I'm your mother."

Don't Go Back to Rockville

PETE BACKS the Volvo out of his mother's driveway. He speeds through the quiet residential streets, takes a left onto Sand Point Way, passes Husky Stadium, crosses the Montlake Bridge to the ramp for 520 West. As he merges onto I-5 he sees dark clouds carrying a streaky gray mist over Queen Anne Hill.

He takes the James Street exit to the County-City Building. Using his security access card, he enters and takes the elevator to the ninth floor. His steps echo in the dark and empty halls. In violation of county policy—priorities are priorities—he uses the DISCUS system to look up an address for personal use.

Back in the Volvo, he rummages through his glove box. Under his Ray-Bans he finds a cassette tape, a compilation of road-trip songs that kicks off with Jonathan Richman and the Modern Lovers—"*Roadrunner once, roadrunner twice, I'm in love with rock and roll . . .*"

Raindrops begin pattering on the windshield as he merges onto I-5 South. He turns on the wipers, which keep a metronome-like beat to "Roadrunner." He was sixteen when he first heard this song.

Pete believes Seattle was a cooler place to live when he was younger, before the 1990s hype, and he believes the country was probably a saner and more civilized place to live before the assassination of President Kennedy, as his mother has told him, and he believes—fears—he may never again feel things with the same freshness and intensity he did that spring with Beth, and so he believes nostalgia is justified, but *what fucking good is it?*

"Roadrunner" is followed by Everclear's "Summerland," which reminds him of the snowy night with Esmé, the Replacements' "Left of the Dial," which reminds him of Beth, Golden Earring's "Radar Love," which reminds him of numerous road trips, Bon Jovi's "Wanted: Dead or Alive," which reminds him of the old MTV, America's "Ventura Highway," which reminds him of Jayne the Canadian, the Plimsouls' "A Million Miles Away," which reminds him of Los Angeles, Led Zeppelin's "Ramble On," the Who's "Goin' Mobile," and Springsteen's "Thunder Road," all of which remind him of adolescence, and of how far he has not come since then.

The low clouds clear and snow-capped Mount Rainier grows in perspective as Pete speeds south. At the Olympia exit, he turns off the stereo to study his map because, of course, maps must be read in silence.

The rain stops by the time he turns down a wide street lined with magnolia trees. The houses are old and well maintained and politely marked with street addresses.

The blue light of dawn is just rising on the horizon and Pete turns off his headlights as he stops in front of a two-story Victorian with a large front porch.

He steps out of the car and stares at the dark windows and drawn curtains. In his limited teenage stalking experience, master bedrooms were usually found in the back, while the children's bedrooms were usually on the street side, but he would rather not risk throwing stones at the wrong window.

Reading a phone number off the computer printout, he punches it in and hopes Esmé has a phone in her bedroom.

Two rings and then a woman's voice answers groggily, "Hello?"

"Esmé?" he says.

"Esmé?" she repeats.

Pete is about to hang up when he hears another female voice on the line. "Hello?"

"It's for you, Esmé," the woman says and hangs up, rattling the phone for a couple seconds before clicking off.

"Hello?"

"Hi, it's me."

"What time is it, Pete?"

"I don't know. Why don't you turn on a light."

"It's five-forty A.M."

"Turn on a light."

"*Why?*"

"Just turn on a light."

"Pete, why are you calling me now?"

"Turn on a light so I know which room is yours."

A moment later the curtain opens in a bedroom on the right corner of the house above the garage and Pete can see Esmé from the waist up, naked, phone in hand, looking out.

"Should you be flashing the neighborhood like that?"

"Oh my God," she says. "What the *hell* are you doing?"

"Visiting. Can I come in?"

"Are you drunk?"

"Not legally."

"Pete, this is an idiotic idea."

"I can see where your room is," he reminds her.

The curtains close.

"Esmé?"

She hangs up the phone.

Pete pulls his Ray-Bans out of the glovebox because the blue light is brightening. He steps out of the car. Robins are chirping, a sound he has not heard in a long time.

He starts across the yard, leaving tracks in the dew, then cuts over to the garage. He swings open the door, pockets his sunglasses, looks into the darkness. A Volvo station wagon and a Saab sedan are surrounded by bicycles, garden hoses, and other suburban miscellany. He spots a stepladder hanging from nails on the wall.

As he walks out, precariously carrying the ladder, he sees Esmé on the front porch in a white terry cloth robe, staring at him.

"*What are you doing?*" she says in something between a whisper and a shriek.

He stops. "I need to see you."

"What happened to your eye?"

"I was at the Sub Pop party. I thought you would be there."

"Were you the one who started all the fighting?"

"*No.*"

"Ssssh. Get in here before you wake my parents," she says, glancing around, "or the rest of the neighborhood."

He steps toward her.

"And please put the ladder back, Sir Lancelot."

Our Day in the Bushes

"DON'T YOU think you're a little old for this?" Esmé says as they tiptoe through the foyer.

"Hey, you're the one who's living with her parents."

"Be *quiet*."

They stealthily climb up a wide wooden staircase, one slow step at a time. The hardwood hallways creak as Pete follows her past a ticking grandfather clock.

We're getting older every goddam minute.

They enter her bedroom, she closes the door.

"Wow," Pete says.

Dominated by pinks and greens, the room is cluttered yet organized: framed photos, a vanity table with etched roses in the mirror's borders, cassettes stacked next to a boombox, and a framed poster of the Space Needle, which Pete's eyes linger on.

"Symbol of the future," he says.

"Yep." She adjusts and tightens her robe. "Are you going to retry Keith?"

Pete shakes his head. "There's nothing left to try—he confessed again, and this time he did it in front of several people—we may even have it on video. Sundfell will have to take whatever we offer."

"And what's that going to be?"

"Rape 3. Not much jail time compared to Rape 2, but it fairly reflects what happened."

"So shouldn't you be celebrating?"

"I am."

Pete continues to look around, feeling the rush you get from being turned on to previously unheard recordings of a favorite band.

He picks up a photo frame with a montage that includes a high school cheerleading squad in full regalia. "You were a cheerleader?"

"Far right edge," she admits.

There she is with pigtails.

"A desperate plea for acceptance and attention." She laughs. "From a past I'm still trying to live down."

Pete picks what he presumes to be her prom photo. "High school boyfriend?"

"Adam," she says. "We had a fun summer, then he went away to college back east. Never heard from him again."

Adam, short-haired and skinny, looks like he's about fourteen. Pete sets the photo down, and picks up one with two young children on a backyard swing set.

"That's me with the nice fat gap in the teeth."

"And who's the handsome fella?"

"Joey. Joey lived next door. We went to kindergarten together. He used to chase me all over the neighborhood, trying to get me to kiss him. Weirdly aggressive for a five-year-old."

"Your first kiss?"

"Nope. I never let him. I was *going* to, eventually." Esmé looks at the photo. "I guess I was waiting for the right time and place. I figured we would eventually have our day in the bushes. But his parents suddenly packed up and moved, so we missed our day."

"Joey's probably a registered sex offender by now."

Esmé takes back the photo and sets it on the vanity.

"Can I smoke in here?" Pete asks.

"No."

With nothing else to do with his hands, he reaches out and takes hers. Though she allows this, her touch feels tentative.

"I want to be with you," he says.

She does not say anything, does not look like she is about to.

"Meeting you threw me," he continues, "and I didn't know what to do about it at first, but now I know. I want to be with you."

"Pete?"

"Yes?"

"We missed it."

"What? What do you mean?"

"I've been thinking about this a lot, and I really don't have it all sorted out, except I know I'm leaving and you're staying here and we missed it, we just *missed* it."

Pete aches for her at this moment.

"Did you listen to CDs or the radio," she asks, "when you were driving here?"

"A cassette."

"From the seventies or eighties? Maybe the early nineties?"

"A collection."

She tilts her head as though a point has been made.

"Have you ever," he says, "had sex on that bed?"

She smiles. "Not with another person."

He kisses her and she kisses him back, but when he puts his arms around her waist and tugs her in, she resists.

"Pete, no. I shouldn't, I can't."

Time to pull out the marriage proposal?

He kisses her again, she pulls back.

"I didn't hear 'I don't want to,' " he says.

"I *do* want to, but I *don't* want the regrets that I know will follow. I don't even think we should *talk* until after I'm settled in at school. I'll e-mail you when I get there."

"I *knew* that e-mail comment was going to haunt me."

"I'm serious. It'll be easier then. I've finally made a right decision, and I want to be able to stick to it."

Pete pauses, his hands on her hips, her hands on his shoulders. They stare at each other for a few beats and suddenly he sees it, he feels it—he's blown it, *she's gone*. He wants her and he's reaching for her, but he's grabbing at empty air.

Better Man

ANGLED LIGHT from the sunrise gleams off the wet street as Pete speeds away from Esmé's. He contends with the morning traffic on I-5, edging past the Tacoma Dome, Emerald Downs, Sea-Tac Airport, Boeing Field.

As he approaches the West Seattle bridge he recalls the days when the band would return from the road ragged and sleep-deprived. The van would cruise over this rise in I-5 and the sky-line would come into full view and the familiar panorama would give him a strong clean rush. He is running on that same adrenaline now.

Traffic begins to bog down at the Mercer Street exit, then slows to stop-and-go as Pete crosses the I-5 bridge over Lake Union. He winds his way in and out of the lanes, probably doubling his travel distance just to keep moving, then takes the Forty-fifth Street exit to the University District.

He cannot find parking in front of Winter's duplex, and as he cruises the neighborhood he does not see her old Mustang.

Eventually he finds a semi-legal spot about a block up from her place. As he walks back down the street he passes a man rolling a large plastic garbage container down his driveway, cursing.

Winter's screen door is locked and so Pete pushes the ringer. He hears the buzz.

No response.

He buzzes again for a four count.

No response.

He buzzes once more, another four count, then pulls out his cell phone.

"Winter," he says to her answering machine, "I have to talk to you. I'm at your place now, but you're apparently not, are you? Okay, call me on my cell when you get the message."

After sleeping in his car for he doesn't know how long, he wakes up to see Winter's Mustang pulling into the spot in front of him by a fire hydrant.

Winter, not yet seeing him, steps around and opens her passenger door. She pulls out a large white cake.

"Winter!" he calls as he approaches.

She turns, holding the cake. "Hey," she says. "What's up?" She's smiling. "Looks like you had fun at the Sub Pop riot."

"What's with the cake?"

"It's from a party last night. I don't even like cake, but Tina was so paranoid about eating it and getting fat she gave it to me." She holds the cake out to him. "Take it."

"Thanks, but no."

"Take it. I want to show you something."

He lets her hand him the cake. She then flips her left hand over in front of his face. His eyes fix on the platinum ring with an emerald-cut diamond and he watches a raindrop hit her finger and trickle over the stone.

"He proposed," she says. "What do you think?"

He hesitates. "What did you say?"

"What do you think I said?"

"I don't know."

"I said, 'Sure.' "

"So you're engaged?"

"That's how it works."

She lowers her hand, smiles at the ring, *beams*.

Pete suddenly realizes he has never seen her so happy.

"I was up all night celebrating with the girls," she says, still staring at the ring. Then she looks back at him. "So what are you doing here? What's up?"

"I just needed to . . . tell you something."

"What?"

"What?"

"Yes, what?"

"That I love you."

She looks at him quizzically, mouth open slightly, wet bangs hanging over her eyebrows, breaking his heart.

In this instant Pete believes he can win her back. He is flush with audacity. This is the stuff of story and song, the boy gets the girl, the two that most need each other end up together. *But . . .*

Semi-rational thought disrupts his confidence as he wonders if this is best for Winter? Is he thinking of anything but his own fears? Has she met a better man, or at least someone who can love her more completely and certainly?

What would Priest Boy advise?

"You love me," she finally says.

"I do."

"And you're telling me now?"

"Yes."

"*Why?* Why now?"

"I just want to . . . wish you well. That's all. That's why I'm here. You've earned every bit of good you find and I hope you find it with this guy. I truly do."

Winter, never stingy with her tears, cries. He kisses her lightly and tastes the salty wetness and doesn't know if it's from him or her.

"I like you this way," she says.

"What way?"

"Kind of emotional."

"I'm going to miss you."

"For a while, yeah, but you'll forget about me soon."

"*That,*" he says, "you're wrong about."

And she was.

Took So Long to Bake It

AFTER WINTER disappears inside, Pete sets the cake on top of a garbage can near his Volvo. For a long moment he watches the frosting melt in the drizzle. This puts him in mind of a song he cannot quite place.

Suddenly his legs are unsteady and he sits on the wet sidewalk, cups his chin in his hand.

What now?

He could start searching for Beth again but, truth be known, that self-comforting illusion is gone for good, and the sadness that hits him is not for this loss, but from the realization that his persistent desire for something lost long ago has cost him other possibilities.

He raises his face to the rain and tries to feel each drop as it makes contact, but there are too many and soon he just gives in to the random tap, tap, tap. Tears form at the edge of his eyes, then release, flowing and merging with the rainwater that rolls down his neck and under his shirt.

"MacArthur Park," that's the song with the damn cake, he suddenly remembers. *Band should have done a cover.*

Traffic is heavy as usual in the U District and Pete nearly causes a wreck as he turns onto the freeway ramp. He hears the honking, but does not know it is directed at him. He is still shaking off his best mistakes.

The sky darkens and the rain thickens as he crosses the I-5 bridge. Suddenly the streetlamps fizz on, flickering from yellow to orange, lighting the bridge like a runway.

Pete clicks on his headlights. In his view ahead is downtown and the Space Needle.

Well, you still have Seattle. Possibilities.

He turns the radio on.

ACKNOWLEDGMENTS

I have never written an Acknowledgments page before, but this novel might not have come to be if it weren't for the friends, colleagues, acquaintances, and strangers I was helped by, inspired by, and/or ripped off. So I want to thank some of them now since I tend to forget to in life: my agents Christy Fletcher and Lucy Stille, my editor Bruce Tracy, Tracy Pattison, Morgan Entrekin, Brian McLendon, Oona Schmid, Dan Rembert, Peter Farrelly, Dario Scardapane, Lori Applebaum, Dennis Ambrose, Lisa Van Atta, Faith Beattie, Alida Becker, Todd and Ruth Black, Kurt Bloch, Bill Block, Jayne C., Tina Davis, Cameron D., Stephanie and Constance Dorgan and all the good folks at the Crocodile, Sarah Ellegood, Bret Easton Ellis, Elliott Bay Books, Gary Fisketjon, Scott Fogg, Richard Ford, Claire F., Lulu Gargiulo, Mary Ann Gwinn, Nathan Hale, Gerry and Angela Harrington, Holly, Phil Joanou, Penny Johnson, Kerin Keller, Scott Lee, Resa, Sean MacPherson, Mike Musburger, Michael Upchurch, Molly Ringwald, Miss Marina Rust, Lee Richards, Bob Simonds, Alexis Smart, Chris and Janet Smith, Adam and Sara Smith, Tracy Sultan, Susie Tennant, Christy T., Binky Urban, Kurt Vonnegut, Kim Warnick and the aforementioned Fastbacks, Meg Watjen, the guys from the poker game at Mr. Sahgal's, everyone at the Pierce County Prosecuting Attorney's office who gave my life a second act, my family, and all the artists who wrote and performed the songs that have kept me alive this long.

ABOUT THE AUTHOR

MARK LINDQUIST was born and raised in Seattle. He is the author of the novels *Sad Movies* (Atlantic Monthly Press's bestselling trade paperback in 1988) and *Carnival Desires*. His books have been published in seven languages. He has written for *The New York Times Book Review, The New York Times Sunday Magazine,* the *Los Angeles Times Book Review, The Seattle Times,* and *Details,* among other publications. Currently he's a deputy prosecutor in the Pierce County Special Assault Unit. Website: www.nevermindnirvana.com